MISS DIRECTION

ANNIE HOLDER

www.annieholder.com

"May they stumble, stage by stage
On an endless Pilgrimage..."
from The Travellers' Curse After Misdirection, by Robert Graves

ONE

Nothing had ever hurt as much as this. No wonder people pleaded, and sobbed, and made foolhardy deals so readily – because they simply couldn't bear this *pain*.

Love is weakness, exploitation; regret – that much is obvious. He'd deliberately never let its poison infect him…and yet it had, hadn't it? Insidiously, he'd fallen in love – without choice, without reason – and barely realised until it was snatched away. What he needs now is the only thing capable of alleviating this unremitting agony: revenge. Though this vengeance is complicated. Not merely an eye for an eye…there's more at stake.

Richard. It hurt to even speak his name! He'd told him – wide-eyed, ingenuous – that he wanted to get off the grift. One last job and he was quitting the con, permanently. But the double-crossing little bastard had lied to him. He'd had no intention of giving up his life of crime. What he'd done was ensure everyone looked the other way while he went after the prize most worth having.

James Chadwick leans his aching head back against the sofa cushions, and briefly closes his eyes. Reams of paper are spread across his lap, the floor, the seat next to him. Richard had died in pursuit of a considerable fortune; the papers strewn around him are the evidence – extensive research, dead ends, cold leads… Forty million sits in an offshore fund, ripe for appropriation…if *only* he could *find* it! Richard had been killed before he could complete his search. The contents of this folder take Jimmy Chadwick so far, and no further. Places he can't go. He needs an agent. A dogged investigator. Someone who will persist despite the obstacles. Someone who also lost everything that fateful December afternoon: a confused, forsaken, betrayed man called Phillip Fishmandatu; once an honest copper, now a fallen angel desperate to be avenged.

****

Phillip Fishmandatu sits on the deck outside his beach bungalow and dangles his legs in the plunge pool up to his knees. The water feels chilly on his skin, its velvety coolness calling him to slide off the t-shirt he's just put on, ease himself in fully, and float...the hot Antiguan sun warming him, and his body casting rippling shadows across the underwater tiles. He resists the temptation; there's work to be done. He looks at his watch. Nearly time.

The heat of the day builds; the relentless sun a pulsating fireball driving even the most dedicated worshipper under their parasol to escape its ferocity. The sand becomes too hot to walk on, and the wood of the poolside decks burns even the hardiest feet. The perfect time to catch them at home.

Catch them...

Fishmandatu smiles sardonically – what a thoroughly apt choice of words.

TWO

Bobbing in the pool, sealed in his blissful bubble, eyes closed, fierce noonday sun cooking his protruding belly, Marc Pickford occasionally lifts a hand to trickle cool water across his hot skin. His somnolent brain decides it's heard a noise, and only then begins idle speculation about what it might have been…perhaps something hitting the tiled floor indoors? That makes him wonder if it's lunchtime, contemplate how peckish he's becoming, and raise his head hopefully. Instead of a picture of pleasing domesticity, he witnesses what he at first assumes is a burglary in progress, as a rangy black man forcefully pins Tammi against the pillar to the left of the kitchen. Panicked – and these days not lauded for his athleticism – Marc leaps for the edge of the pool, misjudges it, slips, and submerges. He ingests a significant quantity of heavily-salted water, and shoots back to the surface spluttering for air. Fruitlessly wiping stinging eyes with wet fingers, he gropes blindly for the side, levering himself heavily upwards to land on his stomach with an ungainly flop, clouting his knee painfully as he wriggles bodily across the red-hot patio.

Tammi's assailant smirks cruelly as he watches Pickford flap around on the scalding tiles like a walrus, scoffing sarcastically, "Here he comes, your Knight in Shining Armour. He might make it off his fat arse sometime in the next fortnight...and then I'm in big trouble, aren't I?"

The slap of Marc's massive feet whacking urgently across the patio causes the intruder to whirl and face the lumbering, dripping, panting, slipping giant lurching over the now treacherously-wet floor. Both men regard one another with awkward recognition and cold calculation, each awaiting the other's first move. When it becomes obvious Marc will not act until he does, her captor abruptly shoves Tammi with all his might towards his adversary. She connects hard with the expanse of obese torso, a sharp smack of bare flesh-on-flesh that makes both gasp, stagger, and slide in the puddle widening from Pickford's sopping body. By the time they've righted themselves, the front door is slamming. The man is gone.

Marc grips Tammi roughly around her upper arms, his wet flesh cold on her warm skin, "What the hell's *he* doing here?!"

Irritably shoving him aside, Tammi pelts down the hallway after the intruder, barking, "Don't just stand there! Get the car keys – *quick*!"

Marc complies with as much urgency as he's capable. They bundle out of the villa and down to their open-sided Landi, zipping up to the development's entrance and waiting an eternity for the wrought-iron automatic gates to swing slowly inward. Livid at the maddening delay, Tammi thumps the dashboard violently, "Come on...come *on*!"

Marc guns the little 4x4 through the gate as soon as it'll fit. Tammi's already flipping open the glove compartment and wiggling out the ancient binoculars. She looks frantically left to right, squeaking, "Stop!"

Marc reacts, swerving the vehicle to a sharp halt on the grass verge just outside the gate, glaring at her, "*Now* what?"

She points, "Look!"

The lithe figure of the man is jogging away down the side of the coast road, a mile ahead at most.

"Come on!" Tammi slides out of the open-sided Jeep, clad only in her bikini, dancing barefoot off the burning tarmac onto the sandy scrub, "Shit, that road's hot! Come on, hurry up! We need to follow him!"

Marc scowls, climbing out unwillingly, leaving a damp outline of his still-wet body on the battered leather seat, "We haven't got any shoes on. Can't we follow him in this?"

Tammi rolls her eyes in exasperation, "At jogging pace? Are you mad? We'll catch him up in twenty seconds, and then what? Hold our bloody breath and hope he doesn't notice *the car* that's cruising three feet behind him? We need to see where he's going...so we've got to follow him with some *subtlety...* Come on, or we'll lose him."

"What if he's walking to his own car half a mile down the road, huh? That buggers up everything, doesn't it?"

Tammi weighs up the risk, "Ok...I see your point... Look, there's parking at the back of the beach, right?"

"Yep."

"If he came here in a car, that'd be a practical place to leave it, wouldn't it – to sneak up to our place on foot...?"

"How did he get onto the development?"

"Oh, Marc, how should *I* know?! Ring a random bell and pretend to be the milkman! Wait in the hedge for someone to drive out, and dive through before the gate shuts? There are a million ways! When someone presses our bell and tells you they've got a delivery, how often do you check the camera before you buzz them in?"

"Well…"

"Exactly! And nor does anyone else, probably. Besides, it doesn't matter where he's *been*! I care about where he's *going*! Come on. We'll just follow him to the beach, and then we'll make a decision from there, ok? He's going round the corner now; we'll lose him! Come *on*, Marc!"

She's off, scurrying down the rough verge after her quarry. Marc sighs resignedly, leans over to tug the key moodily from the Landi's ignition, and follows her.

Past the corner where the road swoops down from the bluff to run parallel with the rugged coast, the man strides across the parking area, the soles of his flip-flops puffing little clouds of sand into the air. He doesn't stop at one of the few vehicles as expected, but continues down onto the beach. They follow at a discreet distance, prudently hugging the undulating dune. Stopping at a suitably-screened vantage point dotted with sapling palms and spreading seagrass, Tammi clamps the heavy plastic of the binoculars to her face, tutting and muttering as she twists the wheel to bring the beach into sharp focus, scanning impatiently until she spots him again, now strolling casually, his green t-shirt bright and noticeable against the white sand.

Hovering annoyingly behind her, Marc rattles out questions she can't answer, "Phil-bloody-Fishmandatu! What's he doing here? How did he know where to find us? What does it *mean*?"

Tammi tries to ignore him, fixing her eyes on the distant, diminishing figure. To shut him up, she snaps, "I don't know what it means!"

"What's he come here for? Why now?"

"I *don't know*, Marc!"

"Didn't you ask him?"

She takes her eyes from Fishmandatu long enough to glare at him, "Funnily enough, we were rather too preoccupied with having a punch-up to manage much smalltalk. I could've done with you five minutes before you chose to make an appearance!"

Emasculated, Marc puffs out his enormous chest, and pompously declares, "I frightened him off, didn't I?"

Tammi's glance is withering, "Don't flatter yourself, I think he was going anyway. He just turned up to rattle my cage…and, to be honest, he's succeeded…"

She moistens dry lips, and squints at the bright green speck of Fishmandatu's t-shirt.

Marc flops dejectedly onto the sand, absently rolling a lone pebble with his big toe, eventually asking, "Can you still see him?"

"Yeah, he's going straight down the shore. Is that deliberate, do you think? So we can watch him if we choose? I mean, we weren't exactly stealthy back there. He must have assumed we'd follow, right?"

Marc shrugs, not really listening.

She exhales irritably, "What's at the other end of this beach?"

"Just that boutique hotel…and then the headland and the hill behind it."

At length, she abandons her observation, "He's gone."

"What now?"

"I don't know…"

"Do you think he's in the hotel?"

"Only one way to find out!"

Afraid of her answer, he ventures tentatively, "What are you going to do, Tammi?"

She taps the binoculars distractedly against her thigh, "I'm going to wait until it gets nice and dark, and go and have a look…"

"*Just* a look?"

Lightly, "Of course, what else?"

Marc swallows apprehensively, "Do you need me to come?"

"I don't think so, do you?"

"No witnesses, eh?"

"I'm not sure what you're implying, Marc…I'm just going to assess the situation."

"What did he say to you in there?"

"He said, *Hello Tammi, remember me?*"

"That was it?"

"Yeah."

"What was that designed to achieve?"

"How many *more* times – I *don't know*, Marc! But I'm going to find out…"

****

Fishmandatu fidgets in the wide bed, kicking to dislodge the sheet that coils uncomfortably about his clammy legs. The ceiling fan spins with a low, hypnotic hum, the displaced air barely stirring the mosquito net around the grand four-poster. Still wired by the events of this afternoon, the dreamworld eventually exerts its beguiling pull and Fishmandatu is more-than-willing to drift, lulled by the drone of the fan and the distant, rhythmic rush and splash of breaking waves.

He knows sleep has fully claimed him when he feels the delightful, fanciful brush of a soft, female body at his back. A dream. Just a dream. A smooth limb curls over his hip, little toes tickling down the front of his shin to rest lightly on the top of his foot. Small breasts squash against his shoulder blade, titillating with delicious, plump pressure. One slim hand snakes around his shoulder, down his chest, and across his stomach to his firming penis; gentle, warm fingers sliding with invigorating rhythm. Fishmandatu sighs, luxuriating in the sensation, knowing it's fantasy, not caring, leaning back and murmuring, "Annelisse..." into the hot darkness. Moist lips nibble his ear, a gentle exhalation of breath tickles tantalisingly as she breathes, "Phillip..."

Fishmandatu twitches involuntarily. Wide awake in an instant, he grabs at the slim wrist and yanks it away, spinning around on hands and knees to face where she lies, smirking, amongst the tumbled covers, clothed only in pale moonlight.

Fishmandatu sinks back onto his heels and scrapes a hot hand down his sweating face, growling, "That was a shitty thing to try."

She sniggers, "I thought I was doing quite well. What gave it away?"

He grunts humourlessly, "Of all the women I've ever known, only my mother calls me Phillip."

Tammi Rivers pulls a face, "Eurgh! No wonder you got up so quick!"

She rolls onto her back, pushing her palms against the headboard and stretching languorously across the mattress, opening her legs deliberately, knowing he's still watching her. It would take so very little to give in to this, to allow his tired and broken brain to pretend that the woman before him is the woman he *so* wants her to be. Not Tammi Rivers, the conniving con-artist with the suspected blood of more than one victim on her hands, but her identical twin – Annelisse – the only woman he's ever really loved. Fists clenching around the bedclothes, he bunches them in his palms until his knuckles ache. It feels as if he teeters on the knife-edge of temptation for a shamefully long time before his conscience drives him backwards off the bed, struggling clumsily from the clutches of sheet and mosquito net.

He staggers across the room, grabs at a pair of shorts, and hurries to conceal his revealing arousal. He plunges into the Antiguan night, crickets chirruping busily in the undergrowth to either side of the bungalow. He totters a few feet across the private deck and subsides onto the furthest sun lounger, legs rubbery with shock. The strength of his desire for her staggers him. She isn't Annelisse, and yet the striking resemblance is seemingly enough for it not to matter to his treacherous body or tormented brain. Only the remaining tatters of his once-enviable integrity hold him in check.

Starting at a sound behind him, there she is, swathed tightly in the discarded bedsheet. He doesn't know what he'll do if she approaches.

Thankfully, she sinks gingerly to the deck in her restrictive, makeshift toga, and edges tentative toes into the plunge pool, "Oooh, chilly!"

The voice isn't identical, but the tone and inflection are close enough to further trouble his fragile emotions. His chest aches as if he's sprinted up a hill. He thought his heart was already broken, so how can it be shattering for a second time? It doesn't seem fair that he's died inside, but is still expected to go on living. Head in hands, he pointedly refuses to look at her, praying she'll leave if denied the oxygen of his attention.

She makes no move to depart. Distractedly, he wonders where her clothes are. She's talking to him. Is it wiser to listen, or blot it out?

"I wanted to get your attention...the way you got mine this afternoon."

Fishmandatu daren't lift his head. He snorts mirthlessly, "Touché. I think we're quits now, don't you?"

No response. He can't help but snarl caustically, "Just out of curiosity, how *did* it feel to spectate at your own funeral?"

Tammi shivers, and wraps her bare arms around her body, "If I'm honest, a bit fucking odd..."

Something in her voice makes Fishmandatu stare searchingly at her. She skilfully avoids eye contact.

Fishmandatu smiles sorrowfully, "I have to admit a grudging admiration for how fast your brain works. I mean, you had everyone after you, and you plucked an escape plan out of thin air, and made it stick! It certainly helped that my department was so endemically-corrupt they didn't actually *want* to solve the case...but you were still exceptionally convincing. You had a plausible answer for everything; pretending to be the distressed Mrs Annelisse Pickford, conned by her own sister, taken hostage at knife-point. You committed two murders and got away scot-free – "

"Hey!" The intangible moment of confessional intimacy is past. She hisses with urgent fury across the few feet of sultry air separating them, "Self-defence! If I hadn't done what I did, do you think Ricky McAllister would have shown any mercy? It was him or me, simple as that. Tell me what else I was supposed to do!"

"I don't know. I wasn't there."

"No, you weren't. You didn't show up and stick your flamin' oar in until it was already way too late."

"And your sister?"

"She *fell*!"

"*You* put her in that risky situation! You're as responsible for her death as you would be if you'd pushed her!"

"I was nowhere *near* her! You know that...you were closer to her than I was. In fact, I seem to remember, Phillip, that you were the one she was trying to reach when she slipped. You. Not me. Arguably, if you'd just left well-alone – instead of meddling in something you didn't understand – both your mistress and your unborn child would still be alive today...and we wouldn't be here having this pleasant little chat."

Strange; she's not the first to insinuate that Detective Sergeant Phillip Fishmandatu, who's previously prided himself on his perception and judgement, was in fact stumbling blindly, pitiably and constantly behind the curve. He'd worked in a department so riddled with corruption it was rotten to the core, yet never noticed there was anything wrong with any of his colleagues. He'd accepted all their explanations at face value until the truth was too glaring to ignore. How had he ever dared call himself a detective?

The torpid night air slowly ripples the water between them. Illuminated by the pool lights, the resultant moving shadows travel across her bare, brown skin like writhing serpents.

Disorientated, he breathes, "You're evil…"

She starts, staring at him in affronted astonishment, retorting, "I'd rather be evil than weak!"

"What does that mean?"

"Annie told me she was already carrying on with you before she married Marc…and went through with the wedding because he was a millionaire, and you weren't. But she kept on using you for her own amusement anyway, didn't she – and you were so pathetic that you *let* her? Now, there's a man with zero self-respect."

Defensive, Fishmandatu blurts, "It wasn't like that! She knew she'd made a mistake marrying Marc – "

"Funny how she only came to that realisation decades later when his money dried up…"

Fishmandatu wrestles with the disquieting accuracy of this analysis, too choked to repudiate.

"We're straying from the point of my visit. I want to know what you're doing here, what lunchtime's little performance was designed to achieve."

"What do you think?"

"I must confess I'm still struggling to work it out. It's not as if coppers who get the push for misconduct can legitimately afford swanky beach bungalows on Caribbean islands, is it?"

"Implying?"

"That you're not paying for this. So who is, and why?"

****

Nathan Palmer nods with fatigue, and tries to keep his wandering attention on what his boss is saying. There's an annoying crackle on the line from London, making it hard to hear, and Jimmy Chadwick's voice is uncharacteristically animated – a world away from his usual sardonic, upper-class drawl – as if the gangster is anxious.

"So, you can see them now, Nathan?"

"Yes, Mr Chadwick." Nathan leans forward again and squints down the powerful telescope to make doubly-sure. You can never be too careful with Chadwick. There's every chance the devious bastard has someone watching the watcher. It never does to promise what you can't deliver, or embellish what you can't prove.

There they are, sure enough; two small, indistinct figures in the muggy darkness, lit eerily from below by the pool lights, "Yes, I can see them right now."

"And they're just sitting there?"

"Yes."

"But you can't hear what they're saying?"

"No, Mr Chadwick. I told you, they're on the deck. The devices I planted in Phil's bungalow can only detect what goes on inside the room. They aren't powerful enough to pick up sounds outside."

"Do you think he knows you've bugged the place, Nathan?"

"No. No way." Nathan recalls the last few days of recordings, eavesdropping on Fishmandatu's frequent nightmares; hearing him call out in his troubled sleep, and be an uncomfortable, unwilling witness to his former colleague's tortured tears, "He has no idea he's under surveillance."

"Splendid. For the time being, I want it to stay that way. You are my insurance policy, you understand? Phillip has his instructions to carry out, and I have no reason to think he won't do so…unless he's led astray in some way."

"Yes, Mr Chadwick."

"It's not Phillip's integrity that's in question, Nathan. I simply have reason to believe the Rivers woman can be…how can I put this…rather *persuasive* when it suits her…?"

Nathan chuckles, and takes a swig of the coffee at his right hand, gagging as he realises it's stone cold, steeling himself to gulp the mouthful.

Chadwick is still purring down the receiver, "I fancy Phillip's not in the correct frame of mind to resist." Nathan thinks of that earlier, desperate groan of desire. It wouldn't take much to tip Fishy over the edge. He's bereft, abandoned, humiliated, lonely… "I'll keep an eye on him, Mr Chadwick."

"Good man, Nathan, good man…and, in your absence, I will, of course, ensure a reciprocally-close eye is kept upon your lovely wife and darling daughter…"

Nathan's insides tighten. He squeezes his eyes shut, bows his head, and fights hard not to puke up the cold coffee he's only just swallowed. For Dionne and Amanda, Detective Sergeant Nathan Palmer sold his soul to this most-urbane of devils. It's impossible now to seek to buy it back. The price is greater than he will ever be able to afford.

"I'm doing everything you asked, Mr Chadwick!"

"Of course you are, Nathan…of course…" The honeyed tones ooze unctuously from the mobile 'phone, and Nathan's senses swim. Queasy with fear, he shivers despite the humidity of the night.

"Keep an eye on him, Nathan. A close eye. I'll be in touch."

The murderer cuts the call, and Nathan flings his 'phone onto the opposite armchair with an exclamation of fruitless rage. He spends a moment or two deep-breathing, slowing his thudding heart. To allow panic to take hold is pointless. He's powerless to control what happens four thousand miles away in London. The message is abundantly clear: do as he's told and Dionne and Amanda will be safe. Disobey, and…? It doesn't bear thinking about, so he buries it. There's no alternative. High on the hillside above the exclusive beach-bungalows of Phillip Fishmandatu's five-star retreat, on the wide, empty poolside of a secluded plantation villa, Nathan Palmer bends once again to the eyepiece of his telescope and settles, as instructed, to keeping the closest of eyes upon his erstwhile best friend…

****

She yawns vocally, eyes scrunched, mouth wide, as if she doesn't care how she appears in front of him because he matters so very little.

"I'm tired…"

He retorts unsympathetically, "You chose to come here in the middle of the night to pull your poor-taste stunt."

Tammi simpers sarcastically, and troubles the surface of the pool with lazy fingers, reawakening the rippling serpents. Fishmandau rubs his glazing eyes. Since his breakdown, disciplining his wandering concentration is a battle he frequently loses. Doubt, fear, desire, fury – all churn his fragile wits and make him feel light-headed with grief and bewilderment.

Rivers yawns again, "Why don't you make me a nice cup of tea, and then we can talk properly, like intelligent human beings who know the score. I'll level with you, and you'll extend me the same courtesy. Perhaps we can put one another out of our individual miseries?"

Fishmandatu doesn't want to make her anything. He doesn't want to sit and pretend civility with the woman who is the cause of all his pain, but he's here to do a job. He has to be professional about it. He'd gone looking for trouble this afternoon; he shouldn't be so surprised he found it. He'll do as she asks. Not because he wants to, but because it's expedient. Shuffling unwillingly to his feet, he pads inside, returning presently with two cups of tea made in the bungalow's basic kitchenette.

He thumps one cup down onto the deck beside her, and stomps moodily back to the safety of his previous seat on the opposite side of the pool. Again, she agitates the water, lifting a languid arm and watching the drips form, swell, and plop from the tips of her relaxed fingers. Conversationally, she remarks, "Awfully nice here, isn't it? I don't miss England at all."

Fishmandatu considers her words. Apart from a vague and omnipresent pain in his solar plexus, which he attributes to the harrowing events of the past two years and prolonged separation from his three sons, he concludes he doesn't miss it much either. Life in this bubble of opulent unreality is very satisfying, as is the prospect of earning a great deal of money from this unusual assignment.

"*Why* are you here, Phillip?"

"Can't a chap have a holiday? I'm recuperating from a serious mental breakdown. Oh, but you know that, don't you, given you were the cause…"

She regards him coolly, "I thought we'd agreed to level with one another? Nice cuppa, slice of straight-talking?"

Stubbornly, Phillip grunts, "I don't remember agreeing to anything of the sort."

Undeterred, she persists, "How much is this place costing: five; six grand a week? What's financing this 'holiday', Phillip? Who's fronting the cash for you to be here, in my face, bursting into my house on a sunny afternoon and roughing me up for fun?"

He gazes steadily at her, and baits, "You wouldn't believe me if I told you."

THREE

"Heard of a bloke called Jimmy Chadwick?"

It's satisfying to see her jaw drop, her eyes widen. Uncertainty flashes across her face. Brazenly, she crows, "No way! No *way*! I don't believe it. *You*, working for the notorious Jimmy Chadwick? You'll have to do better than that, Phillip!"

How to convince her?

"Wait here."

He goes inside to the safe, returning with Ricky McAllister's assiduously-amassed envelope of evidence, withdrawing two particular items from it, and dropping the folder casually onto the sun lounger at her elbow.

She snatches up the packet, scrabbles through it, demands, "Where did you get this?"

Fishmandatu shrugs as if the answer's obvious, "From Chadwick...and *he* got it from McAllister..."

Her eyes flick from side to side, brain calculating rapidly as she examines selected sheets in obvious agitation.

"Believe me now?"

"*When* did you get this?"

"Couple of weeks ago...before he sent me out here." He watches her intently, "Why, seen it before?"

He passes her the smaller of the items he holds. It's a thin, poor-quality reproduction £20 note.

She takes it cautiously, and examines it in the light shining up from the water. She chuckles incredulously, "How did you get hold of *this*? From Chadwick too?"

He grins, "That's my business."

"Fair enough, Phillip. You keep your secrets, and I'll keep mine. How's that for a deal?"

Still grinning, he declares, "I have a choice. You don't."

"Big talker, eh? Got anything to back it up?"

"The full and considerable might of my new employer?"

She regards him thoughtfully, waving the note, "When Ricky got this counterfeit cash off Chadwick, the plan was always to do a runner abroad without paying him for it. Ricky's idea. Always Ricky's bloody ideas…! I told him we wouldn't get away! I told him Chadwick'd come after his hundred grand eventually. Ricky said he couldn't. He said he was powerful, dangerous…but on a police watch list…that he'd be arrested like a shot if he attempted to leave the country. I didn't know how much of it to believe…?"

"What are you fishing for?"

"Information, Phillip. If you're in as deep with Chadwick as you claim, you'll be able to provide it, won't you?"

"He's under suspicion. It's why he keeps such a low profile. We know – " He stops, realising he isn't who he once was, correcting himself, "*They* know what he is, but they can't prove it. He's got so many coppers in his pocket that any attempts to construct prosecution cases against him crumble for lack of evidence. It just…disappears…"

Tammi thinks of the folder in her lap, and where she'd last seen it – on the hallway floor of Marc Pickford's Kentish mansion, next to Ricky's cooling corpse. She wonders who 'disappeared' it from that crime scene and placed it in Chadwick's hands? She recalls how it had looked the first time…identical to this: notes scribbled on scraps torn from pads, random photocopies, reams of internet printouts copiously underlined, highlighted, and liberally-annotated in the margins with Ricky's spidery scrawl. Not a neat, reproduced copy, but rough, ready, raw, and…unique? Chadwick's apparently so confident of his hold over Phillip Fishmandatu, he's seemingly entrusted his only copy!

He's holding out his hand for the folder. Reluctantly, she surrenders it, "Tell me about Chadwick."

"What?"

"Tell me. You know him. I only know the rumours. You want me to be intimidated by him, explain why I should be. From what you say, he's no threat to me. He can't come and get me, right? And he's sent *you* in his stead! No offence, Phillip, but you're hardly the most terrifying option…"

Irrationally stung, he smacks the folder angrily onto the end of his lounger, "I'm not sure how to take that. I'm not here to terrify you. I'm here to persuade you."

Her reply is scornful, "Persuade me of what? To pay him a hundred grand I don't owe? Hand over the cash or my cover's blown? Face it, Phillip, your veracity's been so utterly discredited over the past couple of years, who's going to trust a word you say now? You practically *screamed* the truth into the faces of anyone who'd listen. No one believed you; they just had you sectioned." She shakes her head dismissively, "Sorry, Phillip, but you have no leverage. I won. They believed me and not you. Live with it."

She reaches beneath an overhanging branch of bougainvillea, tugging out a hidden kaftan and slipping it over her head. She stands awkwardly, pulling it down prissily to preserve a modesty she's already squandered, wriggling the enveloping bedsheet to the ground beneath it.

She's going! Abruptly, without even taking leave! She's half way across his private beach before Fishmandatu recovers sufficient presence of mind to squawk, "It's nothing to do with the hundred grand!"

Her body language betrays only exasperation. She isn't frightened of him at all. Her eyes flash irritation as she marches back up the beach, "Then *what*?"

Fishmandatu goes for broke, "He wants the forty million in your offshore account!"

Tammi, usually so accomplished at keeping her nerve, stumbles on her way back up the steps to the deck, wincing as her toes stub the rough stones. Witnessing this delivers Fishmandatu a surge of self-confidence, enabling him to jerk a casual thumb at the bulging packet of paperwork beside the pool, and drawl, "Pointless denying it. It's all in there. Every single bit of evidence but where the money is right now…and that's the bit I'm here to discover."

Her eyes flick restlessly from the folder to his smirking face, "And if I refuse to cooperate, Phillip, what then? Are you here to kill me at Chadwick's behest? Do you know how hard it is to take another life, no matter what the provocation?"

"Annelisse told me you were a trader once. What if I'm not here to kill? What if I'm here to trade?"

"Trade what?"

"Your freedom…for the money."

"But you hate me, Phillip. Surely the last thing you want is for me to go free? What do you get for brokering said deal?"

"A Finders' Fee."

"Paid for out of my money?"

"*Is* it your money?"

"All the while it's still in my account."

"What about the people you stole it from?"

"Prove it."

He smiles complacently, "I don't need to." He points at the folder, "Ricky McAllister's done it for me. I told you, we know everything apart from where the money is."

"Why would I give it to you?"

"Because I'm the friendly advance-party, here to negotiate. Refuse to deal with me, and what follows will be a lot worse."

"I disclose the location of the money, and you destroy me with the contents of that folder anyway, just for fun. The only way to keep myself alive and at liberty is to keep my mouth firmly shut. Funny Chadwick didn't think of that…? How much of a fool is he?"

Fishmandatu pictures the cultured, elegant, self-assured individual with whom he'd conversed at length about this assignment, "He's no fool. He's an incredibly well-educated and intelligent man."

"Have you genuinely met him?"

"I've genuinely met him." Is he boasting about it? Unaccustomed exhilaration surges within him as he contemplates his own daring, "I've shaken his hand!"

She regards him intently, "Come on Phillip...*explain* to me..."

He's amazed how readily he complies, "Meeting him surprised me. He wasn't what I expected. He's an unlikely villain."

"Because? What were you expecting?"

"The traditional thug! The underworld hard man! The sort of bloke I'd arrest on a weekly basis, once upon a time. There's none of that posturing with Chadwick. He's well-spoken. He's...this'll sound funny, but he's...*graceful*. He's groomed. He looks like a barrister, or a stockbroker. He's so respectable, you'd trust him to watch your stuff while you popped to the loo on a train. Rumour has it he went to Eton; to Oxford! They say he moves in exalted circles. Reportedly, he knows peers, politicians, captains of industry – "

"And yet he squirmed in the gutter with slime like McAllister...?"

"I'm only telling you what I saw; what I've heard. You asked me. We've got a gentleman's agreement. I give him what he wants...and he gives me what I want."

"How much is your Finders' Fee?"

"Five per cent of whatever I recover. Five per cent of forty million's a pretty good payday, I'd say. It'll set my boys up for life."

She doesn't miss a beat, "Oh, Phillip, if I've got forty million, it's news to me! That sounds like a Richard McAllister 'Jackanory'. I *might* still have enough to pay your boss his disputed hundred grand

and get him off my back – I'd have to check my accounts – but that's about it." She points to the folder, "Anything else it might say in there is a flight of fancy straight from Ricky's Machiavellian little mind."

"I told you, Tammi, denial's pointless! I have *all* the information I need to take you down. The one thing that can save you is to reveal the location of your fund."

"Even if I had that kind of money – which I don't – nothing would induce me to tell you – "

"Chadwick will have you killed!"

She smiles. It's chilling. "I disagree. You're the one he'll dispose of…for being useless. Seems he's got forty million reasons to keep me alive!"

She lunges for the folder. It takes him a moment to register what's happening. In those vital seconds, she flits past him to leap over the border of seagrass framing the raised deck. He gasps, springing up, making a grab for the hem of the flapping kaftan, catching a glimpse of slim thigh and bare bottom as she flies to land awkwardly in the deceptively-deep, daily-raked sand of his private beach. He's beside her even as she struggles upright, hauling her back by a fistful of excess material, pinioning her in an aggressive embrace, reaching around her body to wrest the folder from her clutches. She kicks frantically. Daggers of pain shoot up his right shin as a swinging heel finds its target. He swears under his breath, sweeping a long leg like an illegal football tackle, toppling her to hands and knees. A squeak of surprise and pain escapes her. He holds her still with a palm flat in the centre of her back, reaching behind him at full stretch to toss the precious folder safely back onto the deck. It slithers across the sun-bleached wood. For a moment, it looks as if it'll slide straight into the pool, before scraping to a halt against one of the lounger legs. An exhalation of relief, and he drops to the sand beside her, pushing her roughly so she collapses. As she scrabbles to recover, he crawls on top of her, straddling her, gripping her flailing arms and pushing them down into the sand. She squirms and grunts with wasted effort. He shoves down hard with hands, feet, knees, pelvis. His supposedly-safely-vanquished erection stirs at the upthrust of her determined little body against his groin. He drops his head, mouth millimetres from her face. She stops wriggling. Her big eyes watch him unblinkingly.

"I'm not going anywhere, Tammi. You and I have two years of unfinished business. You can do it the easy way, or the hard way, but you *will* give me the information I've been sent here to obtain."

Another fruitless spasm of defiance, "Over my dead body!"

Fishmandatu smirks, and writhes against her, making her eyes widen in involuntary alarm, "Let's hope it doesn't come to that, eh?"

The other sheet of paper he'd been clutching has fluttered to the ground a couple of feet away. He risks releasing one of her wrists, lays out full length upon her tensed body, and stretches for it, sweaty fingertips providentially sticking to the glossy surface, enabling him to flick it close enough to pluck from the sand. Her free hand shoves ineffectually against his shoulder as he flattens her, but stops when he eases back up and wafts the picture across her line of vision. Despite the moonlight, it's dark down here on the beach, shaded from the pool lights by the lush seagrass hedge around the deck.

She's unable to discern what the black and grey images indicate. They look like x-rays.

"What's that?"

"The most damning piece of paper of all. The one that'll prevent you getting anywhere near your forty-mill unless you agree to cooperate."

She opens her mouth as if to argue, so he cuts her off, "I'll tell you what this is, Tammi…and then you can have a good old think what you're going to do about it. This, here, is Annelisse Pickford's dental records – yet more suppressed evidence that should have come to light during the so-called 'investigation' that destroyed my career; proof-positive that you stole your twin sister's identity to escape prosecution for fraud, theft, murder, and God knows what else. One word from Chadwick, and this is back in the public domain. The *only* way to prevent it, is to give me what I've come for."

FOUR

Tammi stands over the bed and stares down at the slumbering figure. For four days and nights she's done nothing but work at the problem, turning it this way and that in her head like a kid twisting a Rubix-cube. What has Pickford done but sit on his backside in the sunshine, getting drunk, complaining about the barefaced cheek of Fishmandatu's appearance, and generally being as pointless a collection of atoms as ever? Tammi can't suppress the flash of temper that makes her smack the pillow millimetres from the snoring face.

"Oi!"

"Ugh...what?"

"Are you too hungover for intelligent conversation?"

Marc rolls onto his back and squints up at her, face scrunched, the imprint of a fold in the pillowcase marking a red line across his cheek. The bedroom blinds are drawn; the room stale and dark.

Thickly, he gurgles, "Why do you always want to do things at the crack of dawn?"

Having waited an eternity for him to wake naturally, Tammi snaps, "It's quarter to eleven!"

She stalks to the window and flicks open the blinds, bright sunlight instantly flooding the room. Marc cries out in horror, and throws an arm theatrically across his face like a vampire confronted with the ultimate weapon of life-enhancing daylight, "For God's sake! What are you trying to do, finish me off?"

Reinstating the darkness, Tammi stomps back to stand over the bed, hands on hips, "If only it were that easy!"

Marc ignores her, doesn't bother moving his arm, but smacks his sticky lips, rolls his dehydrated tongue across his furry teeth, and croaks, "Get me a drink will you? My mouth feels like the bottom of a birdcage…"

"If you answer some questions."

"What d'you call this, Guantanamo Bay?"

"Do you want to know what's going on or not?"

Marc sighs. He does want to know… He can't think of a way to get her to tell him without conducting this conversation, so grunts, "Yes, of course I do."

"Right. Fishmandatu *says* he's got evidence that exposes us – the identity swap."

"Says…?"

"He was waving bits of paper around. It was dark; I couldn't see."

"Ohhhh Tammi…it could've been his shopping list for all we know! Do we have to do this now?"

"Yes, we do."

"Why? I can't think straight. My head…"

"Because you're only ever one of two things: drunk or hungover – and I get even less sense out of you when you're drunk."

"Ughhhh….get me a drink, eh? Glass of water? Orange juice?"

"He wants 'incentivising' to keep his trap shut."

"So that's it? Straightforward, boring blackmail? Cash in return for keeping quiet about what he knows?" Marc scoffs contemptuously, "No one believed him two years ago while he was still a copper! Who's going to listen now?"

"I did point that out to him."

"Did you make any sort of bargain?"

"No, I told him to sod off!"

"So, nothing to worry about, then! We could give someone some money to rough him up…make him think twice about trying again, eh?"

"I wouldn't bother with that. It'll come back to bite us."

Marc pouts, "*Why*?"

Tammi pictures the grainy image that may or may not have been an x-ray of her dead sister's dentistry, and justifies hurriedly, "Because, genius, that makes us look double-guilty, doesn't it? At the moment, you and I are the innocent and injured parties, and he is the blackmailing aggressor. I haven't spent the best part of two years doing all this friggin' groundwork to embed us respectably here, for you to blow our cover in two seconds flat by paying one of your backstreet poker buddies to fill-in an unsuspecting English tourist on a dark night! We need a way to get him permanently out of our hair whilst ensuring our conduct remains beyond reproach. The idea is Phillip wakes up one sunny morning to find himself more beautifully framed than the Mona Lisa. You know I'm right. Why do you persist in arguing about every little thing?"

"Because it annoys you, and I find it both entertaining and satisfying."

"How spectacularly petty."

Marc wheedles pathetically, "Get me a glass of water…? Have we got any paracetamol? My head's really banging."

Tammi raises her eyes heavenward, but marches to the kitchen nonetheless, returning presently with a fizzing glass of chilled water, aspirin bouncing and dissolving energetically in the bottom. She eases the blinds half-open and pushes the windows wide, admitting the warm Caribbean breeze and the rushing sound of waves against headland rocks far below. Marc struggles to prop himself up and gulp the bubbling liquid, pulling exaggerated faces at its bitter taste.

Tammi sits cross-legged at the end of the bed, and persists, "I think he's ill, Marc. He definitely lost the plot in England, didn't he? I don't think he's recovered all his lost marbles. I think some rolled away…under the metaphorical sofa forever, know what I mean?"

"How much did he say he wanted? Perhaps we should just pay him off to get rid of him?"

"Impossible. He's demanding millions."

"*What*?!!" Marc surges upright in horror, clutches his thumping skull, and subsides against the headboard again, groaning piteously.

"I told you, he's not the full ticket."

Marc burps, scratches his chest, and murmurs, "It is odd *how* crackers he went. He'd always been such a measured guy. Once he pinged, I didn't recognise my old mate Phil in him at all."

"Stress changes you, in every way."

"Despite him being a champion pain-in-the-arse, I am a bit sorry for him…"

"Tell me about the *real* Phillip Fishmandatu…before all this shit."

Despite his raging hangover, Marc responds with characteristic generosity of spirit, "Oh, great bloke! Good fun. Sense of humour. Very bright. Very...analytical. Worked things out. Uni; sunday mornings, he'd be on the sofa with a bucket of coffee doing those logic puzzles you get in the weekend papers – when the rest of us were so hung over we could barely form sentences! We'd have to watch endless cop shows on the tv. Phil'd always know who-dunnit before the big reveal. We'd all be guessing randomly – it's the butler, it's the wife, it's the bloke who owed him money – and he'd have worked it out from the tenuous clues they crowbar in all the bloody way through! He loved a good mystery. Probably why he became a Detective."

"What was his degree? Psychology or something?"

"No...Geography, I think."

"And yet he became a copper?"

"Not at first. He got some other job out of Uni. Can't remember what. Got married, had a kid...breakneck speed, you know? Then, just as fast, it was all over. He was divorced and out on his ear. He packed in the office job and joined the Met. I think he wanted some structure, some direction...and it was a steady wage and a pension. His family's got bugger-all money – they couldn't help him. He dug in and worked his way up. It got under his skin somehow. He enjoyed it: a new mystery to solve every day."

Tammi watches Marc closely, "And relationships?"

"I think he had some long-term bird on the go, but he never really talked about his personal life. Then, suddenly, he got married for the second time! A girl much younger than him. Had more kids. I assume that marriage ended when he had his breakdown."

"So, he *did* lose everything that mattered to him – career, family, friends, reputation…?"

"I suppose he did. All because he wouldn't shut up about Annie! Why he was so bothered about *my wife*, I'll *never* understand…?"

There are none so blind as those who will not see. Tammi looks pityingly at Marc, but fortunately he doesn't notice. She concludes, "So, he's got nothing; he's worth nothing."

"He's got to be flat-broke. He had virtually no money to start off with. I daresay two divorces have pretty much finished him."

"Would you say he was desperate?"

Marc contemplates the horrific, and thankfully completely hypothetical notion of going without, and volunteers with feeling, "Bloody hell, I would be – wouldn't you?"

Tammi recalls the many privations of the past, despises Marc passionately for causing her to suffer them, and murmurs, "He'd be prepared to risk everything…if he thought he could screw some money out of us?"

"Possibly. I told you, he's not the guy I remember. Last week, bursting in like that…! The look in his eyes…*deranged*!"

"Do you think he'll leave eventually, if we just ignore it?"

"He's come all this way. The last couple of years should've demonstrated to you what an obstinate sod he can be if he thinks he's right. He probably won't give it up without a decent battle."

"Do you think there's any reasoning with him?"

"Who knows these days!"

"But once there was?"

"Phil is methodical…frustratingly so, sometimes. If something doesn't add up, he'll pick and pick until it all unravels. If you can demonstrate to him a reason why…? But he's bonkers now, Tam. He won't listen, will he? He just sits down there on the beach staring at us through his binoculars, tailing us wherever we go! Hardly the behaviour of a rational man! He either thinks something's changed in the last two years that'll give him leverage over us – but I can't see what – or he's at rock bottom and there's nowhere else to go. Win or bust."

Tammi considers an alternative angle to straightforward greed, "Does he love his family?"

"He certainly always loved his kids. He did his best by them…I suppose, until he went barmy…?"

"Hmmmm…." She stands, sliding her feet into flip-flops.

"Where are you going?"

"To strike while the iron's hot. To reel in and reason with a lunatic."

****

Following her to the closest grocery store at the nearby marina, he agonises and hesitates on the pavement opposite, before finally pursuing her inside. This is the closest he's been to her since that night on the deck. Just dwelling on it bewilders him. His face burns with remembered mortification.

Ducking through the fluttering plastic strips of the fly curtain, he enters the cool dimness of the grocery store. Strong scents of rich soil and ripened fruit assail him. Melons, peaches, dusty grapes – all piled in burlap-lined crates. Grubby sweet potatoes in sacks sit pudgily on the tiled floor, leaning up against one another like drunks at a bus stop. Boxes of plantain and bananas wrapped in curling leaves jostle for room with overflowing buckets of chillies and gnarled ginger.

He picks up a plastic basket from the stack by the door and hovers indecisively. The young girl behind the closest cash-register glances at him, pops her chewing gum disdainfully, and turns to serve her next customer with minimal enthusiasm. Not wanting to arouse suspicion, Fishmandatu shoots speedily past the haphazard fresh produce display, and inches around the first shelf of tins, packets, and bottles. No Rivers. He attracts a couple more quizzical looks, so makes an effort not to tiptoe and sneak, but to walk with nonchalance up the first aisle and around the corner. Inch. Peek. Check. Clear. Amble casually up this gangway as well. It occurs to him he should put something in his basket, but doesn't dare take his eyes from the end of the aisle in case she appears. He could just stick out his hand and select at random, but knowing his luck he'll end up with tampons, incontinence pads, or something equally embarrassing. He tries to suppress the nagging conviction he doesn't have a clue what he's doing. What he needs is to be calm and methodical. Start at the very back of the store where the huge freezer cabinets rumble and rattle, and work his way towards the front, flushing her out like prey in long grass. He can then lurk unobserved behind the shelves, watch her through the checkout, and follow her from the shop, choosing exactly the right moment to pounce. Purposeful now, he walks briskly across the worn floor, making for the back of the store. He reaches the freezers, glances left to ensure the aisle is empty, and backtracks speedily down to the next, accidentally kicking a rattling stand of sunglasses with his heel as he reverses, making it waver dangerously. Horrified, he whirls around and grips the rack, trying to steady and silence it. Glancing anxiously left down the closest aisle, there she is, looking his way, seeking the source of the sound! He immediately drops his head, using the peak of his baseball cap to shield his face, making a grab for the first thing he sees in front of him: a glossy bestseller on another rickety revolving tower of fat paperbacks. He pretends to read the blurb intently, cringeing inwardly as he turns it over in his hands and sees it's a *Jilly Cooper* novel with an appropriately-saucy cover design. Not exactly the most macho choice. Cheeks aflame, hands shaking, he forces himself to stare at the novel as if giving it serious consideration, counting to fifty before daring to raise his head again. The aisle is deserted! Cursing under his breath, he fumbles the book back into the overfilled rack with such clumsy force he creases the pages and bends the cover. Like the tower of sunglasses next to it, the rack is precariously topheavy. His rough treatment makes it sway alarmingly, causing him to have to throw his arms around it in a steadying embrace. By the time it's stable and he's managed to shove a couple of suitably-masculine items into his basket, several moments have passed. He's worried she might already be through the checkout! Unconcerned now about appearing erratic in front of the locals, he pelts back down to the front of the shop, skids to a halt behind the first row of shelving, and peeks cautiously around it. No Rivers in the four-deep, eye-rolling queue for the sluggish girl at the till. She'd had a basket of produce. She wouldn't have been able to progress through in the short time he'd taken to stabilise the book rack. She must still be in the shop somewhere. He spins on his heel with a squeak of trainer sole and resumes his chaotic search. She's nowhere to be found. Had she spotted him at the sunglasses, abandoning her basket and running from the shop? Only one thing for it – go back to his bungalow, collect his powerful binoculars, and return to his usual vantage-point on the beach, waiting for her to reappear on her private terrace, accepting he'll have to try again tomorrow, or the day after; secretly relieved to have their next direct encounter postponed by his own bungling.

Tucking his basket surreptitiously at the end of a deserted aisle, he turns to leave the shop, and walks straight into the motionless, smirking figure of Tammi Rivers.

FIVE

An exclamation escapes him. There's no pretending a coincidental meeting. Hot with humiliation, Fishmandatu's shoulders slump and he stands before her like a chastened child, wishing the ground would open up and swallow him.

With the directness he still finds disarming, she remarks mockingly, "Do much tailing of suspects in your old job? Only I think your surveillance technique's a bit rusty. You buying this book or not?"

From the top of the full basket hooked over her forearm, she holds up the damaged paperback, "After all, they can't sell it now…and you're the one who ruined it."

The mischief dancing in her eyes makes Fishmandatu smile despite vowing not to. She giggles, and pushes the book into his unresisting hands, "Come on. We need to pay. I think that's your basket over there, isn't it?"

Sheepishly, he retrieves it from the floor, tosses the paperback in on top, and follows her meekly to the checkout.

Standing outside the shop, the strong late-morning sun bakes their uncovered skin. Mobilettes and rusty old cars bounce past them on the potholed road. Mind blank, Fishmandatu struggles to take the initiative. Teasing gently, she suggests, "In a rush to get home and start your new book, or shall we go for a drink somewhere?"

He gapes, "Really?"

"Well, that 'unfinished business' you're so keen on…we'd better just get it done, hadn't we, as you're becoming a serious irritation."

And he'd thought he was having absolutely no effect whatsoever! "Isn't it a bit early?"

"You're on Island Time now, matey. Stuff happens when it's good and ready."

"Will the bars be open?"

"I think you can have rum for breakfast here." She points down into the marina, "There's a couple of ok places there."

"Right."

They walk a hundred yards in silence before he nudges her arm, indicating the two plastic carrier bags of shopping she shifts from hand to hand as if they're heavy, "You want me to carry those?"

The question brings her up short with wide-eyed amazement, before she shyly averts her gaze and murmurs, "Yes…please…"

Both start, blush, and grin bashfully as he reaches down to relieve her of her burdens and their hot fingers touch.

At the waterside bar, already surprisingly crowded for ten minutes to midday on a late-spring Thursday, Tammi leads him between the gloomy jumble of indoor tables and onto a sun-drenched deck, floating amongst the moored boats in the very centre of the marina. A few plastic chairs and tables are set out, all with umbrellas made of dried palm fronds which rustle like falling rain in the constant Caribbean breeze. She chooses a table beside the water. Sitting here between the large and expensive yachts, bobbing up and down with the motion of the pontoon, it feels very much as if they're on the deck of their own private boat, soaking up the sun and planning where they might sail away to next. The pinging sound of taut ropes on metal masts puts Fishmandatu in mind of distant church bells, carried on the wind across London's rooftops and in through his open bedroom window on a lazy Sunday morning. Suddenly; powerfully, he longs for home.

Where the fabric of his shorts stops, the exposed backs of his thighs stick sweatily to the plastic chair. He wriggles around, sliding to slouch in his seat and extend his feet to rest on the rope barrier between deck and water, setting it swinging gently. Two drinks are brought despite neither of them seeming to place an order. He takes off his cap, rubs at his perspiring forehead with the back of his wrist, and swigs the milky liquid in the glass before him. Coconut, lime, and a hit of rum that could launch a rocket. He blows out his cheeks, eyes wide, alcohol-laced breath catching in the back of his throat. Tammi grins, "Livener?"

"Cor…you could say that!"

Instead of sitting at the table as he'd assumed she would, she instead drags one of the plastic chairs right up to his, seating herself facing him as if they occupy a love seat in a secret bower. Her fingers rest on the arm of her chair, which abuts his so closely he'd only have to roll his arm outward a centimetre to cause their skin to touch.

"Are you enjoying this?"

Taken aback, unsure what she means, he blinks and stares until she snaps, "You're like a randy dog on the Postman's leg; there's no shaking you off!"

He sniggers, and retorts, "I told you, I'm not giving this up! I'm doing it for my boys…and for Annie – " He hesitates, then truthfully admits, "And to prove to myself I still can."

Her intense gaze bores into his, "Phillip, hear me when I say – *I'm not the one in danger here! You* are, regardless of what evidence you hold in your precious folder."

She states this with such confidence he can feel his shaky resolve crumbling. She always speaks as if she knows more than she's letting on. He struggles to remind himself she's all style and no substance. He takes another unwise glug of the rum, which warms his throat and chest like a swallowed tongue of flame. He coughs, gasps, manages to gurgle, "What are you saying?"

"What I said days ago. I'm sure you're a superlative investigator, Phillip…but you won't come through for him when it matters. He needs a bloke who'll go for the jugular when instructed to do so. You haven't the balls, despite telling yourself you're an edgy, tough-guy these days."

"Tammi, you're still not listening! What I've told you will come true. If you refuse to deal with me, I can't protect you from what will follow…to make you comply – "

"What do you *care*?"

"I want to get paid! I *desperately* want to get paid, ok? I've got a lot of making up to do with that money!"

She raises an eyebrow, "Trying to buy her back, Phillip?"

Indignant; frustrated at her deliberate obtuseness, he growls, "No! The money's for my kids! I want to give my sons the sort of opportunities the Marc Pickfords of this world assume are theirs by right! I want to cheat the lottery of birth! I'm going to load the odds in favour of my boys for once!"

"Sounds to me like you're trying to buy them too, Phillip."

"You can think what you bloody well like. I've got a good reason for being here – "

"Yeah, I made you look a fool and your ego can't take it. You're here to beat me at my own game. You've just admitted as much. 'Proving to yourself you still can'…? You won't, though."

Fishmandatu scowls, and takes another huge mouthful of rum. It's odd; his cocktail isn't getting any emptier, yet Tammi's is practically down to the dregs. A milky residue of coconut coats one side of her glass. He can't remember seeing her drink a drop.

"Fine. If you won't deal with me, see how smug you are when Chadwick sends in the professional 'persuaders' and I hand over my file to whoever is most interested in investigating you for fraud, identity theft, embezzlement – "

"Phillip, no one else is coming to take this responsibility off you! Can't you see? He's going to force you to do whatever he wants. He's going to make you do all the things you're privately so worried about. Can you torture me until I finally give up what I know? What if I never do? What if you actually have to kill me? You can't, can you? Inside, you're still a decent, upstanding, law-abiding citizen. You're only here doing this now because you know you can't beat me the honest way. If you could have arrested me that night at Gatwick, you would have done, wouldn't you? You'd never have gone over to the dark side!"

"He can't 'make' me do anything. I'm here of my own volition. We've got an agreement – "

"I'm sure he's very attached to it. Just out of interest, did you tell your army of ex-wives where you were going?"

"What?"

"Did you explain to your kids why you wouldn't see them for a few weeks?"

Puzzled; befuddled, Fishmandatu slurs, "No...I... What...?"

"You just left them all behind, cluelessly, in England – where Chadwick is – with no protection of *any* kind...? No exhortation to watch their backs *at all*?"

"Um – "

"That's how he'll do it, Phillip! I'm sure that's how he gets pretty much everyone. All those coppers you say he's got in his pocket? Didn't advertise 'corrupt situations vacant' in the local paper, did he? I reckon he probably eased them into a compromising position...and tightened the metaphorical vice on their nuts until they came around to his way of thinking. You're fine; no one's coming out here after you. Why bother travelling all this way when he can apply pressure to the tender little bodies you've left behind, within easy reach? How old are your sons, Phillip? Old enough to put up a fight? Even the littlest ones? That's how he gets you: coercion. You commit crime under considerable duress, and then you're his...end of."

A powerful memory assails Phillip Fishmandatu: poor Nathan Palmer's hunted expression as he revealed the truth of his own association with Chadwick. Nathan had to comply, or sacrifice his daughter.   What choice did his ex-police partner have? Fishmandatu's stomach somersaults violently.   He belches, and a bubble of creamy, acidic alcohol surges up the back of his throat into his revolted mouth.   He grimaces and swallows it again, staring out at the impossibly-blue ocean and glaring-white yachts, eyes watering against the unbearable midday brightness, croaking, "My eldest son...he's just getting to grips with his career. He's like I was in my mid-twenties, trying to make something of himself.   My little ones...they're only nine..."

To catch his mumbled words, she cranes towards him on the rocking deck, suddenly passing the point of balance and tipping off the front of the chair. Instinctively, he reaches out to catch her, and she topples sideways over his scooping arm, giggling bashfully; drunkenly, "Ooooh...I think that was a bit too strong...!"

She's soft...and *so warm*...   At such close proximity, through swimming eyes, Fishmandatu's fuddled senses struggle to separate undiminished longing from disconcerting reality. She's on his lap, her arms about his neck, her lips against his ear, "I think you might need to help me..."

He couldn't have let go even if he wanted to. Struggling to his feet, pulling her up with him, the whole world tips and they cling to one another. She's sniggering uncontrollably, "Oh God...no more lunchtime rum!"

Fishmandatu feels unhinged.   Exhilarated, he holds her possessively, far tighter than he needs to. They fumble a shopping bag each.   Weaving back between the close-packed tables is a challenge. The bags tangle about their legs and catch on chair backs.

She seems to find it all irresistibly funny, and Fishmandatu can't prevent the grin that tugs at the corners of his mouth. He's unaware they pass the observing Nathan Palmer by inches, Fishmandatu's bag clouting his one-time buddy around the back of the head as they stagger for the door.

Outside, the street bobs gently up and down as the deck had done. She snuggles in, arms about his waist, body curling to his side like an infant primate to its mother. She's murmuring something. He cups her ringlets in his free hand and tilts her face up to his, "I can help you, Phillip…but only if you help me…"

"How…?"

"I need to know what you know."

"You *do* know what I know! We're about the only people in the *world* who know the full truth – "

"No, Phillip…I mean about *me*. I need to know what you know about me."

"I don't understand – "

"I need to read that folder, Phillip. The one you guard so jealously? I'm happy for you to supervise me doing it…but I can't do anything for your vulnerable little boys without it. I *could* save them from Chadwick's horror. It depends whether or not you actually *want* me to. You might love the lure of money more…I don't know you well enough to tell."

He gasps, horrified she could think so little of him, "I don't! I couldn't! I will never love anything as much as my sons! They're all that keeps me breathing in and out every day…the belief that soon I can make it right for them."

"You know what they really want more than games consoles and iPhones is their Dad back from the brink, right? I'm sure they'd forfeit every Playstation in the world for that."

Fishmandatu's throat tightens. Tears rush into his unfocused eyes, "What can I *do*?"

Clinging to him, she breathes passionately, "Take me back with you! Convince me you're telling me the truth! Give me what I need, and I can make it *all* go away...I *promise*..."

****

Pouring sweat with the effort of beating his quarries home, Nathan skids across the poolside patio and slides into his seat, clamping on his headphones, impatiently waggling the computer mouse to bring the hibernating machine to life, and clicking on the recording software. He slumps back in the chair, taking a much-needed breather and a gagging swig of stale Cola from the open can that's been on the desk all night. He wipes the sweat out of his eyes, and leans forward to peer down the telescope.

No sign.

Where would they go if not back here? What the hell is Fishy up to? It's as if he's completely taken leave of what little sense he's got left! Nathan slouches despairingly, ears ringing with the sound of silence, before petulantly tugging off the headphones and padding to the kitchen for a cold drink. He stands in the open door of the fridge enjoying the cool air swirling around his overheating body – that'll teach him to try and run, uphill, at lunchtime, in the oppressive Caribbean heat – scrolling through the surreptitious pictures he'd taken of Fishmandatu and Rivers in the marina bar, and texting them to Chadwick. Too miserable and weary to hurry, he plods dejectedly back to his post, again sliding on the headphones, wishing he could ring his wife, knowing that's impossible…

A sound rouses him. Nathan's ears strain. He holds his breath. Someone's there…he's certain of it. Yes! The abrasive scrape of sandy shoe on tiled floor. Urgent whispers. Quick, unsteady footsteps. Thuds. A breathy female chuckle. Murmurs and sighs. Are they kissing? Is it Rivers down there with him? It *has* to be! More throaty whispers. More breathy laughter. The protesting squeak of bedsprings. Another soft, seductive female sigh. The low, urgent responding grunt of male arousal. Nothing for a while but the gentlest of muttering…none of the tell-tale gasps and groans of intercourse that Nathan awaits with voyeuristic expectation. Instead, before many more minutes elapse, there's the unmistakeable sound of steady snoring.

The quietest of creaks – someone getting back off the bed? The pat-pat-pat of bare feet across tiles. Nathan clamps both headphones tight to his skull with flat palms, and listens until his head aches. What is going *on*?

The electronic beeps of the room's safe being opened. Rustling of paper. The snoring intensifies. Nothing happens for nearly an hour. Pages turn every so often. No one speaks. Someone snores. Nathan records it all, and doesn't understand what he's eavesdropping upon. Pat-pat-pat again. The reassuringly-solid thud of the safe reclosing. The click of the catch on the French doors, and Rivers flits swiftly across the deck, tramps with effort across the deep sand surrounding the bungalow, and strides out onto the public beach. The shallow waves sweep across her feet as she wanders unhurriedly down the tideline home, a shopping bag in each hand. She appears deep in thought. Nathan watches her for as long as he's able. Unless it's shoved into one of those bags, whatever she took from the safe it's apparent she put straight back – so what was the bloody point of nicking it in the first place? Nathan massages his throbbing temples, and emails the audio file to Chadwick too. He isn't here to think, only to do his master's bidding.

****

"Nathan, do you ever want to see your family again?"

"I – ?"

"What is this horseshit you're sending me?"

"I don't – "

"No information worth *anything*, apart from pictures of yet another sexually-charged encounter, with our boy grinning like the cat who got the cream! How is that in any way designed to keep me abreast of the situation?"

"But the latest file? She got him drunk deliberately! I watched her top up his glass from hers every time he turned his head. She led him on…just so she could get a look in the safe!"

Chadwick responds with weary sarcasm, "Yes, Nathan, all very *Le Carré*… Answer me this – who could possibly have given her the combination but Phillip himself?"

Such an astute observation stops Nathan in his tracks. Fortunately, Chadwick doesn't require any sort of response from his temporarily-dumbstruck employee, "It's abundantly clear from the meagre pickings you've deigned to provide thus far, that young Phillip is having some trouble differentiating between fantasy and reality, and it's glaringly obvious Rivers is using it to her very considerable advantage!"

"He lost it big-time, Mr Chadwick. You know that. The shock...! He lost the love of his life, his unborn baby... He couldn't handle the fact that no one wanted to know the truth about the identity-swap. It drove him crazy. I mean, *proper* crazy!"

"I'm well-aware, Nathan. It's precisely why I chose him for this very particular assignment. Like myself, Phillip has a vested interest in crushing Rivers like a bug...and yet...?"

"He's better, but he's not *right*. He's probably not ready to be here."

"*I* was ready, Nathan. More than ready. I couldn't wait any longer. This is the *perfect* juncture in Phillip's recovery! He's fragile, certainly, but nothing will speed him back to robust mental health like a dose of vindication! Yet, for all that he should hate and despise Rivers as much as she deserves, they seem thick as thieves, and *I'm* the one cut out of the loop! She's being allowed to get into his head...and that is unacceptable on its own, Nathan, without all the other glaring anomalies."

Here, Chadwick pauses, and Nathan realises this time he's *supposed* to say something, "Um...I don't follow...?"

"They never talk inside; have you noticed that? Despite it being much the safest place to converse, wouldn't you say? Less chance of being overhead by a neighbour in a nearby bungalow, or some nosey-parker out on the public beach? Almost as if they've been *warned* not to...?"

Nathan's chest tightens in apprehension as Chadwick continues, "A more suspicious individual might even consider that a plot is being hatched against him by a former partnership seeking to exploit their past association for present gain?"

"I'm not sure what you're implying, Mr Chadwick, but – "

"If I discover you and Fishmandatu are in league with Rivers to put one over on me – "

"You won't!"

"What, Nathan? I won't discover it? You've covered your tracks too well? You're too *clever* for me?"

Frantic, Nathan leaps to his feet, squawking desperate clarification, "No! No! You won't discover it because it's not happening! I'm here at your behest, following your instructions! I've done nothing I haven't been asked to do! I send you everything I get – audio, pictures – "

"And still I *know* nothing, Nathan! Likewise, I *hear* nothing from Phillip. All I receive are your delightful snaps showing Rivers doing what she does best. It's called 'Roping the Mark'…I assume you're familiar with the term? All the while Fishmandatu delays in order to perpetuate his pitiable private fantasies, she learns more and more…and the sensitive information I've sent Phillip to uncover slips further from my grasp. She's buying time, Nathan; any idiot can see that! And Phillip's doing nothing but following his cock up a blind alley!"

"I can't do more than I'm doing without giving away my position. I can't control the fact they talk outside a lot. I definitely haven't told them to! Neither of them has a clue I'm here. *You* told me to stay well-hidden – "

Chadwick's menace freezes Nathan where he stands, despite the ninety-plus Antiguan heat and the four thousand miles of distance from the terrifying murderer, "So I'm forced to trawl through hours of him dreaming, crying, wanking, snoring, farting…and nothing of any use or value because they 'talk outside a lot'?"

"Mr Chadwick, I – "

"You'd better *not* be fucking laughing at me, Nathan Palmer! You and Fishmandatu better *not* be working together. I might be forced to discuss at length with your lovely wife why you seem to have taken leave of your senses at such a delicate stage in proceedings – "

"No, Mr Chadwick, please! I'm doing what you asked; *everything* you asked! Everything I hear, I send you. Everything I see, you see. I've left nothing out; I *swear!*"

"Rivers is clever, Nathan. She's the brightest adversary we've ever faced. She's cunning, aware; adaptable. She's a born survivor. You can be confident she's two steps ahead of us at all times, and we are constantly playing catch-up. I assume Fishmandatu will have told her he is in my employ?"

"Oh yes. That's Phil. Honest to a fault. He'll have told her exactly why he's here, and who sent him. Did you advise him not to?"

"No, Nathan, I gave him free rein to approach this as he saw fit – providing his methods yielded results. To date, they have not."

"Look, Mr Chadwick, if there's one thing you can be sure of, it's Phil's integrity. If you've taken him on to do a job, he'll do it to the best of his ability." Even as he gabbles, Nathan wonders why he's bothering to defend Fishmandatu so vehemently, "He won't be pulling a fast one, honestly! It's not in his DNA to do that. He's straight up. If you can trust anyone on this planet to do what they say they're going to, it's Phil Fishmandatu."

"You're confident of that, Nathan?"

"I'd stake my mortgage on it."

"And what about you?"

"Sorry?"

"Are you 'straight up', Nathan? Experience would indicate otherwise...?"

Fatalistically, Nathan mutters, "It doesn't matter, does it?"

"What makes you say that?" amusement tinges the plummy drawl. Nathan clenches his free hand into a fist and thumps his own thigh, wishing it was Chadwick's face, "If I don't come through for you, shit happens...right?"

Jimmy chuckles throatily, and Nathan suppresses the sudden urge to scream his futile fury into the sizzling afternoon sky.

"I'm in, Mr Chadwick. Well in, and you know it. I will do what you ask. I *always* do what you ask. That's been our arrangement for so long now I can't remember what it was like before..."

"Halcyon days, I daresay," mutters Jimmy sarcastically, "And I'm sure you've never enjoyed your succession of fancy cars, expensive foreign holidays, or your daughter's pricey education one little bit."

"I do what I do...and you do what you do...and it turns the cogs in the big machine. Don't ask me to say whether I like it or not. I benefit materially, for which I am grateful, up to a point. That point being where comfort bisects conscience. Sorry, but that's the way it is. I have regrets."

"My heart bleeds. Can we return to the pressing problem of Phillip Fishmandatu? What are you going to do about your staggering lack of success with regard to close observation of your old pal?"

Nathan calculates feverishly. There is something he can do. He doesn't want to, but…

"I'll give him a nudge."

"A 'nudge'?"

"I can speed him up. He won't know it's me. He'll just comprehend he's being monitored. If he's got any sense, it'll be the kick up the arse he needs."

"And if he's losing all reason in the face of Rivers' manipulation?"

"Then…I'm not sure what more I can do."

"Ah…a shame, Nathan…given the price your darling daughter will pay for your failure."

"Please…Mr Chadwick…I'll get this done! I will! Give me a couple of days. I'll get Phil's mind back on the job."

"Two days, Nathan…and I want to see action, or – "

"You will, Mr Chadwick, don't worry! I'll shake him out of his stupor."

"I'm delighted to hear it. You may have been tasked with watching Phillip…but be very aware, Nathan, that *I* am watching *you*."

SIX

The unfamiliar vibration jerks him awake. He instinctively slaps a palm down on his thigh as if a giant mosquito has crawled up the leg of his shorts. It's only when his fingers connect with the mobile 'phone that he remembers, fumbling it out and staring at it uncomprehendingly.

A text message.

Jimmy Chadwick had given him this 'phone, along with an envelope of single-use SIMs. Who can this message possibly be from but him?

It's oppressively hot. The French doors to the deck are closed. He pushes to hands and knees and hangs his foggy head. This morning's sketchy. Too nervous for breakfast, he'd gone without; then consumed that reckless rum cocktail on an empty stomach in the lunchtime sun.

He listens. The bungalow is silent. Rivers is gone. He feels destabilised by his hazy recollection of events. He stands too quickly, tottering unsteadily for the bathroom as the room tips alarmingly. God, he needs a sandwich or something! His first priority is the safe. The door's firmly shut. He types the release code, opens it, and checks the contents. His passport. The envelope of SIM cards. The folder of evidence. He picks it up and flicks swiftly through it. It all seems to be there, including the vitally-important dental records. She'd kept her word – just to read it and nothing else. Relieved, his next concern is to empty his protesting bladder. He recalls the text, wonders absently what's up, flushes the toilet, fishes the 'phone from his pocket again, and sits down on the closed seat.

'I'm tired of waiting for results that don't materialise. This isn't a holiday; it's an assignment I expect you to take seriously. I suggest you make some progress – quickly – or I will take the necessary steps to speed you up.'

There's a second unread message beneath the first. Fishmandatu opens this too. It's a video. If this message had been from anyone else – his eldest son, an ex-workmate – he'd assume it was one of those stupid *YouTube* gag reels where idiots fall over skateboarding, topple off ladders cutting the hedge, or something equally banal. Usually, he deletes that sort of thing straight away, pompously considering it beneath his intellect. On this occasion, he delays. He simply can't picture Jimmy Chadwick sharing a chummy blooper clip as if they're old mates…so what's this amateur movie all about? Average quality footage shot on a mobile 'phone, probably from inside a car – then it becomes abundantly clear *what* he's looking at, and *why*. It's a film of his wife collecting his two youngest sons from the gates of their primary school. The camera follows their departing figures down the London street for as long as the lens can focus. The meaning of the message and the movie together are staggeringly clear.

Fishmandatu's chest tightens so instantaneously he's convinced it's a heart attack. He can hardly breathe. He grips the 'phone in his right hand, and clutches at his breast with the left. It's some moments before he brings his panic attack under control. Body spasming violently with the physical manifestation of his terror, eyes swimming with running perspiration and coursing tears, it takes Fishmandatu's wavering fingers an inordinate length of time to successfully dial his estranged wife's number. It rings, and rings, and rings…while he sweats, and shakes, and whimpers. Eventually, the answerphone kicks in and Fishmandatu blurts, "Jo, it's me! It's Phil! I need to talk to you! It's *urgent*! Call me back. No…no…you *can't* call me back… I'll call you, ok? *I'll* call *you*. I…I… Shit!"

He's suddenly remembered his presence here is a secret, and the 'phone he's been given isn't meant for contact with anyone but its owner. He severs the connection, cradles the handset against his stomach, and wonders anxiously whether there's any way Chadwick can trace the foolhardy call. What if it puts Jonelle and the boys in even greater danger? Eyes tight shut, he tries deep-breathing, needing to get a grip on his rampant dread. The calming image Providence gifts him is of a floating deck where sunlight sparkles on blue ocean, and makes expensive white yachts gleam blindingly. Unable to stand the brightness, he turns his face to the relief of the shade…and familiar eyes bore into his. *'You just left them all behind in England, with no protection of any kind…'*

Rivers is right. Chadwick got him where he wanted him by flattery and persuasion – and now he's beginning to tighten the screws. Before he knows it, he'll be as thoroughly corrupted as the wretched Nathan Palmer, any remaining dignity and self-respect lost to the ceaseless struggle for survival.

Phillip Fishmandatu doesn't get around to the sandwich that might have helped settle his biliously-churning guts. Instead, he leaves the bungalow at a gallop, racing down the public beach like pursued prey.

Nathan sits back from the telescope and sighs heavily. A horrible thing to do to someone he'd once been happy to call a friend – but what choice does he have? His 'nudge' has got Fishy moving and, right now, that's what matters.

****

It's time to get out of Antigua – that much is obvious. At leisure to thoroughly absorb the full, troubling contents of the folder as Fishmandatu slept off his liquid lunch, the only sensible conclusion is flight over fight. To retaliate, she needs something on Chadwick – and there's nothing! You can't apply leverage to a ghost. If she knew *anything* about him beyond rumour and hearsay…! The one she *can* reach is Fishmandatu, so she must continue applying the pressure to him instead. It's certainly working, just not fast enough. In the meantime, there are those illuminating x-rays, that damning Pathology report on the dead body with its four-month foetus, the comprehensive financial information flippin' Richard pain-in-the-arse McAllister so efficiently chronicled. *All* that evidence cataloguing a career of misdeed! Can she manipulate Phillip into handing over the folder, or will that be a step too far even for a man so psychologically-shattered?

Chadwick wants her forty-million…but Tammi's not so sure financial gain was ever Fishmandatu's primary motive for accepting this assignment. Whatever Phillip might claim, and however creatively he's choosing to kid himself; she's convinced, in his heart, he's still crusading for justice on her dead twin's behalf. Will he really give up so easily on the truth?

Tammi slides off the edge of the pool and into the water, shockingly cold on her too-hot skin. She floats…legs and arms spread in a star shape. Her long hair swirls out from her head like tendrils of seaweed caught in a current. She shivers, simultaneously baked and chilled by intense sun and cool water. What to *do*…? She rolls over and swims a lazy breaststroke to the furthest edge of the infinity pool, leaning her forearms on the moulded lip and her chin on her hands, kicking gently now and again to stop her body drifting away from the side. The hazy outlines of St Kitts and Nevis are visible on the horizon. They look close enough to swim to. Escape *is* possible; simple, even! It's the evidence trail they'll leave behind that troubles her. She's *got* to get that folder – and in a way that provokes no retaliation.

Deep in thought, she's utterly unprepared for the dark shadow that abruptly lunges up from the seaward side of the boundary wall, suddenly blocking out the sun!

SEVEN

Firm fingers grip her wrist. She gasps, flailing backwards, unable to pull free. She goes under, salted water shooting up her nose, stretching toes instinctively finding the bottom of the pool and thrusting back to the surface again. Sinuses burning, she splutters and sneezes but doesn't stop pushing her free hand and frantic feet against the side, still seeking to tug her pinioned arm loose. Her assailant moves in response to her struggles until he's no longer a faceless black silhouette framed by a corona of sunlight. He's just Phillip Fishmandatu.

Flooded with relief, followed swiftly by exasperation, Tammi pulls more determinedly than ever – but he clings on tight. She pants, "What are you doing here?"

His voice is hard, tight; a low growl of aggression, "Is Marc home?"

Is this about the safe? Now he's sobered up, is he regretting his ready accession to her demands? She whines, "Why can't you use the front door like normal people?" struggling on, frustrated and angry, "Let go of me!"

"Is Marc here, or what?!"

"No…what are you *doing* here?"

He releases her. She rubs her bruising wrist frantically, dunking it repeatedly in the cool water to ease the burning pain of pulled and twisted skin. He's trying to climb up from the cliff below onto the side of the pool, gripping its moulded edges and searching below for a foothold to propel himself up. He's whispering urgently, "I need to talk to you!"

Horrified, Tammi shoves him back with both hands, leaving soaking-wet palm prints on the chest of his t-shirt, "You're not coming up here! What if one of the neighbours sees?"

Fishmandatu gapes at her, unable to believe what he's hearing, "This isn't surburbia!"

"Yes it is! That's exactly what it is! Just as much net-curtain-twitching goes on here as in the Home Counties, I can assure you!"

"Tammi, I urgently need to talk to you!"

"You talked to me two hours ago! Have you forgotten that already? It's not my fault you can't handle your drink."

Fishmandatu lets this go...mostly because he can't refute her assertion with any degree of confidence. He still isn't quite sure what *did* happen...

"Things have changed since earlier. Everything's changed! I need to have a serious discussion with you – "

Tammi fakes a pantomime yawn, "The latest in a long line of 'serious discussions'. When will you realise they have absolutely no effect – "

"Tammi, I'm prepared to make a trade! I want to! Nothing to do with Chadwick...a trade between *us*!"

Nonplussed, Tammi frowns in incomprehension, "Eh?"

He holds up a 'phone.

"I can't touch that, can I? I'm all wet!"

"Just *look*."

A video is playing. A poor-quality film of a young woman meeting two little boys and walking with them down the road, smiling indulgently as they exhibit all the normal after-school antics of running, pushing, leaping, chasing, and generally revelling in delightful freedom.

Fishmandatu's voice shakes as he explains, "That's my wife. Those are my two youngest boys. This video is from Chadwick…it came through on a 'phone he gave me…and, this!"

He shows her the text message. Tammi absorbs the information in expressionless silence. It's monstrously-disturbing that it elicits no reaction whatsoever. Is she really so utterly devoid of empathy? Unnerved, he demands, "Well?"

"Well what?"

"Have you no *compassion*? They're *kids*! They're *nine*!"

She shrugs, "I didn't create this situation, Phillip. You did."

"But… But…"

"I did tell you this would happen. Encouragingly, it seems he hasn't done anything to them yet…?"

"No…no…not yet…but the implication is clear, isn't it? I need to give him something, pronto! I've got nothing, Tammi. You've given me *nothing*!"

"Again, not my fault. Yours. You've so far failed to persuade me to take you at all seriously. Look at this morning! You cave under the slightest pressure. I never realised you were such a *whinger*, Phillip! You honestly believe the world owes you a favour, don't you?"

A flash of temper courses through him. He wants to slap her supercilious little face; to grab her head and slam it against the side; to hold her under the clear water until she submits to him. Instead, he grips the edge of the pool and talks himself down from the perilous brink. Hit her, and this is over. She'll never help him.

"*Please*, Tammi. I am here to trade. Please let me come up."

"No!"

She kicks to the edge again, hauling herself half out of the water and craning over the side. The pool cantilevers over the rocks within which its foundations are embedded. She can't make out the narrow, concealed ledge Fishmandatu is standing on. All she can see is the clifftop; scrubby seaside plants sprouting from ancient volcanic fissures, seabirds riding the thermals to their precarious nests…and the foaming, crashing waves thumping the base of the headland a hundred feet below.

"*How* did you get up here?"

Tammi Rivers, who's not afraid of gangsters, policemen, the weight of authority, or the confines of convention, is evidently terrified of heights. Fishmandatu smirks despite his agitation, and states economically, "I climbed."

A particularly-large and well-timed wave thuds into the mouth of the smuggler's cavern far below, echoing up inside the arched cathedral of rock local legends claim can conceal a pirate galleon, reaching their ears like the boom from a distant cannon. Tammi pales visibly, and offers in a small voice, "I'll come down to you."

Fishmandatu savours the rare opportunity to dish out the disdain rather than perpetually being on the receiving end of it, "You *sure*?"

His derision motivates her straight up onto the edge of the pool, straddling the lip, gripping on tight with fists and knees, assessing the surprising secret ledge beneath, and the precipitous but clearly-visible path snaking away between the rocks and down, down, down towards the public beach far below. She regards Fishmandatu scornfully, "Climbed, eh?"

It still requires a considerable leap of faith to tilt her body towards danger, dropping the seaward leg to feel for a foothold. The precariousness of her perch delivers a vivid memory: straddling the safety rail around the airport multi-storey watching her sister's splaying legs bridge the gap between two huge buildings, heels dropping, toes slipping, helpless body plunging into the darkness, lost forever.

A spasm of terror freezes Tammi in place. She can neither climb down to the rocky ledge, nor tip back into the pool. Time seems to stand still…until hot hands, abrasive with sand, grip her thigh; her hips; guiding her to the metal mesh she can use like a ladder. Two or three makeshift rungs dig painfully into the arches of her bare feet, and she's down – terra firma – the soil burning-hot on her uncovered soles. Legs like jelly, she sinks slowly to hands and knees, not daring to look to her right and the open sea, squeezing her eyes tight shut and feeling her crawling way through the nearest suitable gap in the haphazard nest of protruding steels under the pool overhang. Even if she falls forward, a victim of the involuntary vertigo that's making her head spin, the mesh will prevent her rolling straight across the narrow path and plunging over the side. Curling herself around one upright pile like a sloth clutches a branch, not caring about the rust that stains her bare, wet stomach and inner thighs, she admits, "I'm not too good with heights."

The gap she got through is tiny. Fishmandatu drops onto his stomach and commando-crawls forward until he's as close as he can get without becoming wedged. He can't sit up as she can, so tips onto his side and props his head on one elbow. His body's completely in shadow, but from mid-thigh down his long legs protrude out across the path, cooking in the sun. It crosses his mind that if this was a cartoon, poor, hapless Wil E Coyote would trip over his legs and go head first off the cliff while his Roadrunner nemesis proceeded unharmed. The similarity strikes him: Tammi Rivers, endlessly pursued but never captured – and him; metaphorically squashed under tumbling anvils, flattened by falling pianos, blown up by TNT, pulling a ripcord to find no parachute.

She's talking. He listens to her uncharacteristically-meek utterance, "I was halfway over, and it suddenly made me think of that night...the car park roof..."

Phillip says nothing, because what's going through his deranged head is Wil E Coyote running in mid-air – the way only a doomed cartoon character can – before recognising there's no ground beneath his feet, sharing a knowing glance with his gleeful audience, and plunging comically out of shot. It's a moment before he realises, somewhat sheepishly, that she's scrutinising him closely. He worries about the expression that might have been on his face.

"You don't miss her as much as you once did, do you?"

Fishmandatu rushes to justify the absence of emotion, "It suddenly feels as if she's been gone a long time; that a lot's happened..."

Tammi nods equably, "She has been gone a long time. Nearly two years."

"Do you miss her?"

"No. She was a source of considerable frustration."

Fishmandatu smiles sorrowfully, "Yeah, she was. Irresistible frustration…"

"What do you expect *me* to do about your problem, Phillip?"

"I don't know," he confesses simply, "You just always seem to be able to survive. I wondered if there's a deal we could strike. You're right, I did agree to come here mostly just to beat you…because I was 'good' and you were 'bad'; because I knew the truth, but no one cared about it. No one gave a toss about Annie's memory but me! There were too many vested interests at stake for anyone to give a shit what really happened! Our baby went unacknowledged, and unmourned."

She mutters, "Welcome to the real world, Phillip."

"I need someone to help my kids. I don't know how…but you do! You said so in the bar!"

"I said that so you'd let me read your folder! Honestly, you're the most gullible bloke I've ever met. How did you function as a copper for so long?"

"Believe me, these last couple of years, I've been asking myself the same question. I treated the whole thing like my very own detective show. I was playing at cops and robbers. It wasn't serious, because it wasn't happening to me and mine. Now it is!"

Tammi ponders, face resting against the oxidised coating of the metal pile she clings to, tiny flakes of rust sticking to her rounded cheeks like dark red freckles, "We need something sufficiently slow to buy time, whilst still seeming plausible. What we need is to stay Chadwick's hand long enough to escape. There *is* a way. Well, there are probably a million ways, but my blancmange of a brain can only think of one."

"That's one more than mine."

Almost to herself, she mutters, "It's complicated, and convoluted…but legitimately so…*persuasively* so…"

"Are you going to explain what you're wittering on about?"

"I'm not 'wittering', Phillip; I'm thinking…but you're a man, so I'll forgive you for not recognising the signs."

Fishmandatu sneers sarcastically at the stereotypical character-assassination of his sex, and she sniggers at his sulky expression, "By George, I think she's got it! A jolly wheeze I reckon could work a charm. I'll tell you…*if* you agree to stay the hell away from me and my money once we both leave Antigua…oh, and on departure, you'll give me that folder you're babysitting so solicitously. After all, you're never going to need it again, are you." He hesitates. She fills the silence, "You can't hurt me, can you, Phillip? Because of Annie. We both know you won't be able to go through with anything because every time you lift your hand to strike me, you'll see her face. And if you can't hurt me, you can't force me to cooperate. Chadwick will find out you've failed, and then what?"

Fishmandatu shakes his head. He doesn't know. He doesn't want to know.

"He'll rip out your kids' fingernails, one by one. He'll probably accompany that with another adorable home-movie. He might even post the evidence to you Federal Express...probably still with the blood on."

Fishmandatu clamps his hands over his ears, and shuts his eyes, "Shut up! Shut *UP*! Words; that's *all* you've got! You don't *know* what he'll do. All you do is *talk*..."

Tammi jeers, "Why are you so bothered...if it's 'only words'? Way I see it, you've got two choices: fuck off out of my face right now, and your kids take their chances...or you agree to my terms. I'll help your family. I've got money. I can buy some one-way plane tickets, some decent hotel rooms. If you love them, what I'm offering should be a no-brainer. I can also provide a compelling distraction that'll keep Chadwick looking the wrong way while we get you and yours to safety. In return, *all* I'm asking is you give me my life back. I get that folder and the opportunity to deal with it as I see fit. I take it it's the only copy?"

"As far as I know..."

"Very trusting of him just to give it straight to you?"

"I suppose he thought I'd need all the information to adequately conduct my investigation on his behalf. I guess he assumed I'd never let it go, given how much I hate you."

"And that's true, isn't it?"

He smiles wryly, "Turns out I love my boys more than I despise you, Tammi Rivers. Who knew, eh? I thought nothing could be more powerful than the visceral hatred I harbour towards you – for all that you did; for all that you stand for. Turns out I was mistaken."

Sagely, she pronounces, "Guilt is the strongest driver of all."

"*I'm* not guilty! *You're* the guilty one!"

"In the eyes of the law, maybe…but not in my own head, and that's where it matters. That's where it eats away at you until you can no longer recognise yourself, isn't it, Phillip? So, do we have a deal, or not?"

EIGHT

Tammi chuckles. Simplicity itself! She can't believe the mental contortions she's put herself through to arrive here, when the solution's been right under her nose the whole time! Use the resources you have and the connections you've got. All that *effort* reinventing the wheel, when she should have immediately utilised the considerable might of the *existing* Stocker-Pickford family machine!

It's four in the morning. Tammi sits at the dining table, the glow from the screen of Marc Pickford's laptop the only light in the dark villa. Marc's snoring rumbles from the bedroom like distant thunder. Tammi smiles to herself. She'll use the vehicle most-commonly employed by the Stocker-Pickfords to clean up questionable money from overseas; what those in the know call a 'staged dispute'. Two companies: one English; one foreign. Company A 'loans' money to Company B – but Company B defaults on the loan. Peeved, respectable directors of Company A (in this case, the eminently-suitable Stocker-Pickford brothers) take naughty little Company B to court. Naturally, they win. Company B gets slapped with a UK court ruling ordering them to pay, so they do. In comes the 'debt', all shiny and clean; protected from any hint of dodgy dealing by the unassailable legal ruling. There's a court order behind the movement of the money, so it can't be laundered; it must be legit! It's perfect for her purposes! It's particularly ideal for

Chadwick, guaranteeing him the anonymity he neurotically craves. To convince Chadwick she's serious, Company B has to be her offshore entity, although she'll falsify the documents concerning its location. Company A can be Marc's high-risk, high-reward fund named 'Excalibur' – given she suspects the Pickfords do this all the time. Who'll notice another set of court papers shuffled in amongst the existing pile. From what she understands, elder brother Geoffrey leans on his Establishment contacts to expedite the paperwork, and Marc's investment funds distribute the cash with swift efficiency.

Tammi can't stop grinning. This is the fun bit; the mischief she's always loved making. She'll set Fishmandatu up as a fictitious investor in Excalibur. It'll then be up to him to pass the 'loan repayments' he receives from Company B on to Chadwick – but what she and Fishmandatu have agreed is that no cash will ever come. What Phillip clearly hasn't thought through in the midst of his desperation, is the only obvious conclusion the gangster can draw as a result of this deception: that Fishmandatu – the hapless middle-man – has pinched his money.

She'll do what she promised; provide Fishmandatu's family with flights and hotels somewhere sufficiently far from Chadwick's long reach, but that's all. If Phillip hasn't the sense to shift for himself thereafter…? She and Marc will be long gone from Antigua – and the precious folder will be hers. Almost *too* easy! And to think she'd been so worried about leaving an evidence trail behind her! One 'phone call after Fishmandatu left this afternoon, and their new passports are already underway. You can get anything if you know where to look.

A few mouse-clicks, a creative bit of paperwork, a legal form or two, and her input in this charade will be complete. Convincing Chadwick is up to Fishmandatu, but it should be a formality. The gangster's getting what he wants, without being implicated in any way. Fishmandatu is absorbing all the risk on his behalf, and, as far as he's aware, Phillip still retains their fall-back dossier containing sufficient damning evidence to put her away for the rest of her life! Chadwick must surely believe he's won? String him along for a few more days at most, and this latest nightmare will be behind her.

She won't tell Marc they're leaving until they're actually outside the airport. It's better that way. His drunken tongue involuntarily seeks to lighten its load when overburdened with weighty truths. There's a lot below the surface they haven't addressed, because it's easier not to – why go digging for pain there's no need to uproot – but sometimes she wishes they could just sit and really talk about it all, without either of them needing to emerge as victor from every bruising exchange.

She shakes her head, frustration mingling with the regret, and opens Marc's desktop 'Funds' folder. She selects 'Excalibur' and scrolls the investor list. Deep in concentration, she's looking for a suitably long-term customer, whose individual records will likely contain all the documents she'll require to forge Fishmandatu the necessary veneer of legitimacy. Her eyes flick down the right of the screen, reading the file creation dates. This'll do – a client folder opened in the late Nineties, and modified within the last six months. This chap's been on the books so long he'll definitely have all the right paperwork to cover every petty legislative eventuality. Her eyes flick briefly left, largely incurious as to the name, absorbing it unconsciously.

So busy is she with racing ahead that realisation is slow to dawn. When it arrives, her whole body jerks involuntarily, fingers catching at the mouse and clattering it several inches across the table. She freezes, holds her breath, and listens for Marc.

His snores rumble on, their rhythm unbroken.

Tammi yanks the laptop closer, as if those extra three inches have somehow impeded her eyesight – but there's no mistake. Open-mouthed, she stares; incredulous. What are the *chances*...?! Is she reading too much into this? Is it mere coincidence, or the greatest stroke of good fortune since her identical twin's passport dropped into her desperate lap? The name on the harmless little yellow client folder, chosen virtually at random from amongst all the others on that busy screen?

JAMES CHADWICK.

****

She pushes one of the SIM cards, opportunistically-stolen from the envelope in Fishmandatu's safe, into her mobile 'phone. At random, she chooses from a list of numbers written at the top of her sheet of paper. She intends to give each a maximum of four unanswered rings, cut the call, and try another – but the first connects, rings once, and is answered. Before the male voice on the other end can speak again, she blurts, "Want something big? Money laundering via the Met, on behalf of organised crime?"

"Who is this?"

"You can't possibly think I'm going to answer that question."

"If I can't identify my source, how can I verify my story?"

"If I have to give a name, the call's over, the story's dead. I'll ring one of your competitors. I have all their numbers."

"No! Don't do that. You can talk to me. But you know for publication I'll need something I can prove."

"I can give you plenty enough for verification, trust me. Are you recording or making notes?"

"Both."

"Very thorough. Ok. I'll talk, you listen. A couple of years ago, a woman called Tamise Rivers died falling off the top of one of Gatwick airport's multi-storeys. Present at the scene was a Met copper called Phillip Fishmandatu. He was subsequently dismissed for misconduct, for his possible involvement in her allegedly not-so-accidental demise. Rivers was reportedly up to her eyeballs in London gangland…and the latest rumour on the block is that the very same copper's emerged in the employ of a nasty bastard called Jimmy Chadwick. An unusual crook, so they say. Urbane, well-spoken; a proper toff. Ask around. People will have heard of him. Very recently, ex-cop Fishmandatu's been cited as a creditor in a UK court case. An offshore entity's been ordered to settle outstanding loan repayments to a UK investment fund. You tell me if this seems fishy or not, 'cos it whiffs like Grimsby Docks from where I'm sitting – a co-Director of said offshore fund? One 'Miss T Rivers' (deceased)."

"Co-Director, you said. Who's the other?"

"Call yourself an investigative journalist? I'm not doing your whole job for you."

"Names! I need names!"

"I believe I've given them to you. Start with the death of Tamise Rivers at Gatwick Airport, December before last. All the players are on that stage." She glances at her watch. Approaching three minutes' call duration. She needs to get off the 'phone.

"How did you come by this information? Do you work in the justice system? At the Met? What's your source?"

Tammi smirks, "My sauce? Usually tomato, I'd say…unless it's an omelette. Then I prefer brown."

She cuts the call with a flourish, stares at the blank 'phone screen for a second or two, then wrestles the back off the handset, releases the battery with a flick of her fingernail, prises out the stolen SIM, and pushes it very firmly into the wet sand next to her leg. She rips her memory-jogging script into minute pieces, and leans over the ridge of sand upon which she lies, sprinkling the confetti onto the surface of the Caribbean Sea a few feet below, watching with satisfaction as the tiny, white squares soak up the salty water and sink from sight.

NINE

"Boss…you busy?"

"Problem?"

"Not exactly…"

"But?"

The investigative journalist slides around the Editor's door, and eases it shut behind him, lowering his voice nonetheless, "If I were to say the words Stocker-Pickford to you…?"

The Editor cuts him off with a brusque, "No!"

"But – "

"*No*. Every time we go for that corrupt bastard, we end up in the Libel Court. Whatever you've got on the repulsive old reptile, my advice is put it through the shredder, twice!"

"What if it's not him?"

"Eh?"

"What if it's the sons…?"

"What?"

"Bent coppers and alleged gangsters on one side, and the Pickford boys providing the veneer of respectability on the other?"

The Editor's eyes dart to the closed door, and back to his reporter, "Sit down."

The younger man obeys with alacrity.

"Where has this come from?"

"Anonymous tip."

"In that case, forget it! If you've got nothing on-the-record – "

"What if it's deep and detailed enough to run a speculative piece?"

"No! Blair Stocker-Pickford always wins!"

"But it's not Sir Blair this time, honestly! He isn't even mentioned. *I'm* talking about the Honourable Geoffrey Stocker-Pickford M P, and his baby brother Marcus, *the* high-flying investment whizzkid of the 1990s!"

"What's the story?"

"It's complicated…but that doesn't mean it isn't true…"

His boss leans forward, sensing potential, "Is this political?"

"Strictly speaking, no…but it could have serious implications for Geoffrey's future Cabinet career."

"Explain."

"A couple of years ago, a Met copper called Phillip Fishmandatu was dismissed for misconduct – "

"So far, so routine…"

"Yeah…but his dismissal seems to have been the direct result of his mishandling of a hostage situation involving – get this – Marcus Pickford's wife and her sister. The sister wound up dead. Marc and Annelisse Pickford left the country pretty swiftly thereafter, and Detective Sergeant Fishmandatu got kicked off the Force with egg on his face. All very dull, really…*until* you find out Marc Pickford went to University with this Fishmandatu-chap, and the bloke's recently left the UK for Antigua."

"So?"

"Guess where Mr and Mrs Pickford legged it to before the dust had even settled…?"

"Antigua, by any chance?"

The journalist grins, "My anonymous source told me the dead sister was up to her neck in London gangland – and suggested ex-copper Fishmandatu is in the employ of a major underworld player; a guy called Jimmy Chadwick. No evidence as to whether he had links to Chadwick while he was still at the Met, or if this is a new career he's embarked upon since he's had some time on his hands."

"Any way of proving this?"

"Not really…but there's more."

"Which is?"

"My source told me to dig through court paperwork. Sure enough, there's evidence of a loan default between an offshore fund and a UK investment entity called 'Excalibur'. Its Directors?"

"Enlighten me."

"Marcus and Geoffrey Stocker-Pickford. And the offshore fund – guess who *its* two Directors are?"

"Well?"

"The late Tamise Rivers, sister of Annelisse Pickford…and none other than *Marcus* Pickford!"

"So, Marc Pickford had his sister-in-law done away with by a bent copper, so he could pinch her money and transfer it to the UK?"

"It could be that…?"

"Or?"

"On the court paperwork, the offshore entity's been ordered to pay Excalibur. One investor in particular, in fact; the apparent injured party, named as Phillip Fishmandatu."

"Payment for a job well-done?"

"I don't think it's that. Phillip Fishmandatu isn't actually an investor in Excalibur, not as far as I can discover – regardless of what the court paperwork says. But a chap called James Chadwick *is*. He's a recipient of fund dividends going back more than twenty years. He's put regular money in…but he's had a shedload more back out again."

"So, James Chadwick, long-term Excalibur investor, is 'Jimmy' Chadwick, alleged organised criminal?"

"I don't know, Boss. That's the bit I can't prove. Word on the street is that gangster Jimmy Chadwick is some kind of toff – proper posh, and downright evil with it. Now, Geoffrey Stocker-Pickford went to both Eton and Oxford with a boy called James Chadwick. There's no *evidence* they're the same guy…but…?"

"The implication is that the Stocker-Pickford brothers are washing dodgy cash for gangsters."

"Here's the way I see it. Tamise Rivers is coerced (by Fishmandatu?) into making her brother-in-law a Director of her offshore fund. She's then 'removed' by this copper, who, let's face it, is ideally-placed to get the job done. It's speculation on my part, of course, but say the bungling he was sacked over was planned from the start? Say he's simply done exactly what he was told by his gangland boss – all so this Jimmy Chadwick can get his hands on the money in the offshore account…and the Pickfords are helping him do it, no doubt for a fat commission. Big brother Geoffrey uses and abuses his position and his contacts to cheat the UK legal proceedings. Baby brother Marcus provides the financial conduit. In flows the dirty cash, cleaned up by a British court order, no less!

Minimal digging on my part already suggests it's not the first time the Pickford brothers have exploited this particular loophole."

"Flippin' heck! But you have no idea who your source is?"

"Female. Relatively well-spoken. London accent. That's all I've got. I pushed for more…didn't get anywhere, despite telling her if she wanted me to print it, I needed detail."

"Anything on the 'phone number?"

"Course not! Use once and chuck away, probably."

"This is dynamite! The best yet! You know, I got into left-wing journalism in the seventies to expose the corruption of the Establishment. Forty years, man and boy, and the closest I've ever got is fruitlessly pleading the truth in Libel hearings…before the Paper invariably loses because the judge went to the same Oxbridge college as the upper-class arsehole bringing the suit against us. The upshot being, the Big Cheese has to keep getting his cheque book out, and it pisses him off. Without a named source, this time won't be any different, I guarantee it."

"But I *can* report fact, can't I? Stuff that's already in the public domain?"

"Such as?"

"Everything I've just told you! The existence of an investment entity called Excalibur, and who its investors and Directors are. The details of the Phillip Fishmandatu police-dismissal case. His long-term links to Marcus Pickford…and, by association, the not-so-great leap to Geoffrey, a serving M P!"

"None of that is news!"

"It could be?"

"It isn't! No matter how you word it, no one cares about the Old-Boys' network. This is Britain. Discrimination by class is a fact of life. The *story* is the Stocker-Pickford boys money laundering for gangsters – and *we can't print it*! Sir Blair's lawyers will take the whole paper down if we do."

"But – "

"You need proof, not hearsay."

"So public opinion counts for nothing any more?"

"What?"

"Can't we print what we've unearthed, and let our readers decide?"

"It's libellous!"

"It's not, though, is it? I never said alleged gangster 'Jimmy Chadwick' is *definitely* the Excalibur investor and Geoffrey's old school chum *James*. Nor did I suggest this case was anything other than a bundle of amazing coincidences! I listed facts, all of which are easy enough for anyone to check. Based on those facts, *you* put two and two together and extrapolated your theory. We don't have to print anything remotely libellous to get our audience to reach the same conclusions you did, do we? Public outrage at the alleged abuse of privilege! Questions asked, yet again, about the true morality of the Stocker-Pickford clan! Scandal! Members of Parliament mixed up with gangsters!"

"What's new? Money speaks to power."

"Well, maybe, but it's never been so clearly spelt-out in a daily newspaper before."

"I can already feel Sir Blair's solicitors sharpening their quills – "

"No, it won't happen!"

"MPs money-laundering for high-class crooks?"

"Yeah, but all we'll *actually* say is, 'isn't it funny how neatly all this stuff slots together'?"

The Boss chews the end of his pencil, and gives it serious consideration, "All right. I might regret this, but…see where it takes you. Fact-check *everything*, and draft me a feature article for Saturday… Wait!"

"Boss?"

"Not a solitary syllable is being typeset until the Legal boys have been through it with a fine-tooth comb, understand?"

"Perfectly."

"This could be bigger than the Expenses Scandal and the Paradise Papers all rolled into one! If this is our one chance to sink the whole bloody lot of 'em, let's not mess it up."

"I won't, Boss, don't worry. I'll make it *so* watertight, not even Sir Blair's sharks'll find a way in!"

TEN

"It just takes some careful setting up and some precise timing. Your job is to sound plausible on the 'phone and do as you're told."

"Understood. What do we do about moving the family? Do you handle that too?"

"They're your family, not mine! I'm giving you the flights, the hotel...I'm not wiping your arse for you as well. I told you, you're the convincer!"

"I thought you meant of Chadwick."

"I do...but I mean of your family too. If you can't get them to an airport and onto a plane, I won't be held responsible for the consequences. If Chadwick's getting impatient, you need to ring him this afternoon, and sell our arrangement to him in the most persuasive language possible – but first you ring your family, just in case he's not as utterly-convinced as we want him to be."

"What can I tell them?"

"Say whatever you think'll get 'em moving with appropriate urgency...but it's imperative you choose the right person to call. You need a single trustworthy point of contact in England, who can marshal everyone for a swift getaway. The one person who'll comprehend the gravity of the situation and act accordingly. The one you can trust to follow instructions to the letter. I don't want any mavericks freestyling here, thinking they can handle this better than I can – because they can't. Are we clear?"

"Crystal. I'll call Simone."

"Wife?"

"Ex-wife."

"Why not wife?"

"Because my current wife hates me a lot more than my ex-wife does."

"Jesus, Phillip, your life's a fucking disaster area."

He checks his watch. The UK is five hours' ahead. Simone should be home from work by now. He'll ring her mobile and hope she's alone. He walks to the desk by the window, watching the afternoon sun glitter on the inviting surface of the plunge pool. Sighing heavily, he turns his back on temptation, holds the old-fashioned, chunky plastic receiver to his ear, and requests an outside line from the polite Receptionist. He dials Simone before the fear he can taste in the back of his throat stops his mouth like a dose of hemlock.

****

High on the hillside above the bungalow, Nathan Palmer's finger hovers over the mouse button on the laptop recording software. Fishy's calling the UK on the hotel 'phone...so he isn't ringing Chadwick. As Fishmandatu's call connects, Nathan makes his split-second decision. He clicks *stop*, and the recording ceases. A moment of paralysing dread at the enormity of what he's just done, before he robotically starts a second recording. He can explain away a momentary break in the timeline if he has to. Why else begin a fresh file for this call? He's simply covering his arse, isn't he? Nathan drags a clammy palm across the fabric of his t-shirt, seeking to dry it. Noticing the hand shaking, he clasps both together in his lap and sits quite still in his chair as if in silent meditation, while his brain whirrs at a million miles an hour. If he chooses to 'misplace' the second recording, he'll have a note of its duration, and will therefore know exactly how much footage he'll need to exchange for incongruous sounds of Phil's erratic slumber, or the roar of the chambermaid's vacuum – useful noises of which he's already made precautionary copies, just in case.

He takes stock of what he's actually done, seeking to suppress the panic circling his head. So far, nothing untoward has occurred but the accidental cessation of one recording, and the almost-instantaneous resumption of another. He could have fallen asleep, sneezed with his finger on the mouse, popped to the loo at the wrong moment, experienced some sort of power cut. He's sure he can come up with an explanation even the perennially-suspicious Chadwick will accept. It's the next step Nathan honestly can't believe he's contemplating – withholding material he knows full-well Jimmy Chadwick will very, very, *very* much want to hear. Why? He doesn't owe Phil anything. He has the wellbeing of his wife and daughter to consider. Knowingly deceiving Chadwick as good as kills him, and condemns his beautiful girls to God only knows what fate. What's made him press *stop*? Is it no more than an instinctive twitch over which he has little conscious control, or a deliberate act of supreme bravery? Is Nathan Palmer about to prove himself selfless hero, or suicidal fool?

****

A few crackling rings on the other end, a moment's delay during which he hears a rush of background babble – the radio or tv – and then Simone's familiar voice, caution in her tone because she doesn't recognise the number.

"Hello?"

"Sim. It's me."

"Phil? Is this a new number? Where are you, the line's terrible!"

"Um…abroad…"

"Abroad where? What is going on, Phil? Reece says he's been trying to ring you and he can't get through – "

"Sim – "

"He says he leaves messages and you don't return them."

"Sim – "

"He's tried texting you…emailing…"

"*Sim!*"

"It's upsetting him, Phil! You can't behave like this. You're still his Dad. You can't wash your hands of him just because he's grown up – "

"SIMONE!"

"What?"

"Just…shut up for twenty seconds, will you?"

"There's no need to be like that!"

"Well, how am I supposed to explain anything to you if you won't even stop to draw bloody breath?"

"I don't have to listen to this! I know life's been tough for you since losing your job and everything, but I care about my son – "

"*Our* son."

"Well…if you think that, you've got a funny way of showing it!"

"*Please* Sim, just cut me a bit of slack will you?"

"Why should I? Everything's always about people bending over backwards to accommodate *you*! It's high time you grew up and realised you have people in this world who *want* to rely on you – and you persistently let them down! Reece is hurt, Phil! Your Mum can't understand why you never ring her. She's worried about you. What about Jonelle? What about the boys? What poison do you think she's dripping into their ears every day about what an irresponsible, childish arsehole their Daddy is? And she's not wrong, is she? She has every right to tell her sons you've let them down; you've let *everyone* down. Disappearing off, not telling anyone where you're going, never calling the people who give a shit about you. Do you think that's ok?"

"Of course I don't."

"Why are you doing it then?"

"Sim, please – "

"Come on, the smooth-talker who always has an answer for everything! What's your story, Phil? Feed me some suave bullshit and I'll decide how much of it to believe…"

"Sim, *please* – "

"If you beg for my indulgence one more time, Phillip Joseph Fishmandatu, I am slamming this 'phone down!"

"No, Sim, wait! I'm in big fucking trouble! I need help! I need *your* help!"

"What?"

"I know how much I've done wrong, you don't have to lecture me. I'm very well-aware of what a shit father I'm being right now. Believe me, I've got my reasons for the radio-silence."

"Phil, what's going on? Where are you?"

"I'm...in the Caribbean."

"You're *what*?"

"I took a job, Sim. It was supposed to be a one-time thing, and a seriously-fat paycheque. It would've been enough to set us all up for life...but I was naïve. In my defence, I've not been well...I've not been thinking clearly. I just saw the opportunities, but I didn't consider the risks. It's...backfired, Sim... I've put myself in a lot of danger. Worse than that; unwittingly, I've put all of you in a lot more."

"*What?!*"

"Only you can help me get out of this. I've got some money here. I've got a chance to break away – "

"What are you talking about? Start making sense!"

"The job I took was some investigative work. Like a P I...but... Not legit, Sim. I've been working for a bloke called Jimmy Chadwick – "

A sharp intake of breath on the other end of the line. Of course Simone knows the name. Everyone in their area of London knows the name.

"You've heard of him, right?"

"Oh yeah, I've heard of him. He's the guy who burned Christine Fuller's husband's hair off with a cigarette lighter, because the guy owed him money and couldn't pay. He offered him his car, but

Chadwick didn't want that. He wanted to make an example of him –
so he set him on fire. You know that boy, Rashford Peters, who
used to play Sunday Football with Reece…the one who's in a
wheelchair now?"

"Yeah…?"

"The story goes, he got into dealing drugs for Chadwick…and he
creamed too much off the top. They say Chadwick chucked him out
of an upstairs window."

Fishmandatu's guts plunge into his boots. His legs give way. He
isn't quick enough to tug out the chair beside him, so just crumples
to the floor in front of the desk, forehead resting against the sticky,
overpolished wood of the chair back.

In horrified tones, Simone breathes, "Did you actually have a
breakdown at all, or was it just a lie?"

"I did have a breakdown, Sim. I lost my way… Then, I got this
gig because – "

Fishmandatu suddenly pictures Annelisse Pickford throwing back
her head and laughing, and realises it's a step too far to tell his first
wife that all this mess is because he put his mistress before his
second family.

He's shamed by the unconcealed weariness in Simone's voice,
"Just get on with what you rang to tell me, Phil – and then I'll decide
if I think it's so much bullshit or not."

His immediate impulse is to argue with her – but there's no
defending the indefensible. He swallows his pride, and states
simply, "Chadwick employed me to do a job here. It…hasn't gone
according to plan. He's tired of waiting for results I can't generate.

I'm unable to keep stringing him along indefinitely. He's started sending me threats. He's got…oh God…he's got people watching Jo and the boys – "

"*What?!*"

"He's sent me video of Jo collecting them from school…someone following them down the road towards home…"

"Jesus! You stupid bastard! I may not be her best mate, but what have any of them done to deserve that?!"

"I didn't think – "

"No, you just 'took a little job' for the most dangerous bloke our side of the River, and thought it would be fine? You, of all people! Who should know *exactly* how dangerous he is! What fucking *planet* are you on, Phil?!"

"I was being paid serious money! Five percent of forty million quid, Sim! Two *million* pounds! I could have turned all our lives around – "

"Working for a fucking *crook*? I know we were young, but when we met, you had the steadiest moral compass of anyone I'd ever known! What *happened* to you, Phil?"

He thinks, '*Annelisse Pickford happened…*'

Meekly, he whispers, "I made a mistake."

"Too right you did! And now it seems we've all got to pay for it! Same old selfish Phil. As long as you get what you want – "

"*No!* The money was to make amends."

"What utter shite you talk. You thought, rather than put in the effort, you'd just buy off everyone you treated like dirt?"

"No! I thought I could use it to improve all our lives! No more struggle. I wanted to give the boys...*all* the boys, the things I never had when I was growing up. I'm not trying to buy love. I would have given you the money whether any of you wanted to see me again or not. I was doing it by way of apology...an apology going back twenty years..."

"A genuine sorry face-to-face would carry more weight – especially to our son."

"And he'll get it. You'll all get it...but only if we can get the family out...and for that I need you."

"Wait...are you trying to tell me that if we don't leave London, our totally innocent, law-abiding, hard-working son will be the next young man to wind up in a wheelchair – through absolutely no fault of his own – because of something his idiot father's done?"

Fishmandatu gulps, and gurgles, "Pretty much."

Simone makes a noise on the other end of the 'phone that's halfway between gasp of horror and scream of agony. It tugs at Fishmandatu's soul. He cries out desperately, "If it's any consolation, they'll come for me too."

"Not if I get you first!"

"Sim – "

"Why have you dumped this problem in *my* lap, you arsehole? Why do you do this every time? Fuck up, and then expect someone else to fix it?"

"Because I'm stuck here, and you are there. Because I know I can trust you implicitly. Because I know I can reason with you, no matter how much you despise me. Please, Sim. This is for the twins, for Reece."

"*What* are you asking me to do?"

"Convince the family – the *whole* family – to get on the flights that have been organised for them, and not to argue. If they don't, it's all over. I mean it, Sim."

"How can I tell your mother she's going to be murdered if she doesn't drop everything and leave the country? Her head'll explode! And you mean leave for good, don't you? What about furniture, books, clothes – ?"

"Leave it. Sell it. It means nothing if we're all dead, does it? I'll replace everything, I promise. Just bring Reece's baby pictures."

"What about my job? What about Reece's job? He's got a promotion in the pipeline, you know. What about this flat? You're telling me we have to walk away from work, home, friends – ?"

"Yes, that is exactly what I'm saying…or take your chances, Sim. Simple as that. No promotion's worth floating down the Thames in concrete wellies, is it?"

"Oh my God, oh my God…"

"Sim…please…you can't lose it. I can't trust anyone but you to sort this. I can provide the escape-route, the finance, but you need to get everybody to the airport. You need to convince them that going's the only option."

"How can I? What do I say? They won't take me seriously!"

"I've had an idea about that. You don't tell them anything at all about the risk. You tell them I've won the lottery, and we're all going to a secret location to meet up and have the best holiday in the history of the world, ever. They can have anything they want. I've won a life-changing amount, and I want to use it for everyone's benefit…they can all get their hands on their share if they come to see me…"

"Like Jonelle'll agree to that!"

"Promise her an obscene amount of money if she brings the boys to me. She'll come. She believes I owe her…and she's right. I owe all of you."

"And when we get wherever it is we're going, they'll discover there's nothing, you lied to them, and they can't go home. What then, Phil?"

"They will be *alive*. If none of them speak to me ever again, at least I saved them. I'll know I did everything I possibly could…and we can look after each other! We can rely on one another like we should do anyway – like a family."

"Sometimes I want to punch you, Phil! We *had* a family, remember? We had a flat, a marriage, a baby. *You* got bored of it, and wanted out. Then, you had another family – a younger wife, a bigger house, *two* babies this time – but that wasn't exciting enough either, so you got yourself mixed up in a load of crap I will never understand, lost your marbles and your job, screwed up completely…and now we're all having to leave behind everything we know and love and 'start again as a family' because *you* fucked up! *We* didn't! We're doing just *fine*!"

"Sim, you *have* to come!"

"I'm going to come, you prick, because I value my life and the life of my son…but that doesn't mean that anything you've done has impressed me one iota! It doesn't mean you are forgiven for being selfish, and childish, and short-sighted, and arrogant, and – "

"Ok, Sim, I get it! Help me, please, and I promise I will do everything in my power to make the last twenty years up to you. Everything I can, Sim. I mean it."

"You'd better, Phil, and not to me. I made up my mind a long time ago what I think and feel about your behaviour. The people you owe apologies to are your Mum, your Dad, your sons, Jonelle…"

"I would like to be able to change how you feel about me too."

"We'll discuss it, Phil. Don't expect me to just melt in a puddle at your feet like I did at nineteen. I'm a little wiser to you these days. What happens now?"

"Go and get a new 'phone. Text that number to this number. Everyone else junks their 'phones. Even Reece. Non-negotiable. Put 'em down a drain. Chuck 'em in the river. We need to fly below the radar here. We have a matter of hours to play with. Be careful. Be unpredictable. Be aware. Be close-mouthed. Be on that plane. Pack up whatever you can carry and leave the rest. Get to Jonelle's. Sit on her sofa and spit out the lottery story. Don't take no for an answer. I'm relying on you, Sim. I can't do this without you."

"I'm definitely going to punch you when I see you, Phillip Fishmandatu. I might even take a leaf out of Chadwick's book and lob you through a window myself."

"I adore you Simone. You were my first true love, and you'll be my last."

"Get fucked, you disingenuous bastard."

Lying on the cool tiles of the living room floor, headphones clamped to his ears, long wire trailing back to the laptop on the far table, Nathan Palmer holds his hands up in front of his face and watches how they tremble. He's sent the excuse of a laptop issue he's trying to resolve. He can't call home, Chadwick has his 'phones bugged – there's no way to get a message to his girls. So far, Chadwick hasn't contacted him about the alleged technical gremlins, but that doesn't mean he's ok with it. That's why Nathan wants to call – just to check – and also why he can't. Too suspicious. Too coincidental. If he withholds more footage without additional contact or further explanation, it's over for sure. The years of obedient service won't count for anything. He's not concerned for himself – he knew at the very start of this his life would be forfeit one day – but his girls…! The vivacious, bright, beautiful daughter he and Dionne had waited so long for. His patient, calm, supportive, totally-trusting, blissfully-ignorant wife, who thought he did so well financially through a combination of dedicated overtime and special assignments.

Why has his bloody conscience chosen to resurface now, here, when he has the simplest job of all to do – just listen, record, and not get involved? He still has time to pull himself out of this. He can simply send the sound files he's withheld, say he's fixed the glitch, and swiftly bring Chadwick up to speed…but he doesn't move. He remains on the cool floor, watching his elevated hands shake, silent tears of mingled terror and regret tipping from the corners of his eyes and trickling into his sideburns. Listening. Just listening.

ELEVEN

He isn't imagining it. The soft thud suggests the impact of feet upon the enclosed rear deck that houses his outdoor shower. That means someone's taken the trouble to scale the high fencing designed to shield his naked body from prying eyes, hauling themselves up the twisting branches of passion fruit coiling and winding through the trellised woodwork. Who'd climb into his shower in the middle of the night?

Fishmandatu listens to the smooth roll and click of the releasing latch, the slight rattle of the turning bathroom doorknob, the light *pat-pat-pat* of soft shoes up the dressing room corridor towards the main open-plan area of the bungalow. He eases upright as silently as possible, stomach muscles tight. The old-fashioned wooden bed creaks if you move too sharply. He's stretching for the bedside light, fingers millimetres from the switch, eyes on the far corner of the room, when the dark shape abruptly rounds the wall and charges the bed, leaping bodily onto Fishmandatu, carrying swathes of mosquito net before it. Bony knees jab painfully into Phillip's groin. The intruder's face pushes against the swagged netting uncomfortably close to his. Stale breath and rank sweat assail his nostrils, and one clammy hand smacks across his mouth. Fishmandatu clamps his lips shut to avoid accidentally tasting another man's skin. The rough nylon of the mosquito net scratches unpleasantly at his face. He closes his eyes and tenses for the blow Tammi had prophesied would finish him with businesslike efficiency. How had Chadwick worked it all out from the one 'phone call this afternoon, in which he'd shared nothing but irrefutable fact with his paranoid new employer?

When no strike comes, Fishmandatu opens his eyes and stares up into the face of his attacker. It's hard to see – the room's dark, the quantity of mosquito net bundled across him impedes clear vision – but the figure is too familiar not to recognise. Convulsing with shock, his cry of indignation muffled by the suffocating pressure of the alien palm, Fishmandatu tries to wrestle free. The introduction of a large flick-knife into his field of vision swiftly stops the ineffectual squirming.

A cautioning finger to the lips, the man slides off him, stands before the bed, extends the knife threateningly, and indicates that his prisoner should obey. Rubbing his aching wrists, Fishmandatu complies, pushing the rough mosquito netting aside and easing to his feet. The bedsheet drops away and he stands naked and uncertain before the motionless trespasser.

The intruder points towards the French doors, intimating with a jerk of the knife that Fishmandatu should get moving. He hesitates, shyly indicating his nudity. The lip curls nastily, and Fishmandatu finds himself yanked roughly round by his upper arm, and pushed firmly towards the door. The cold of the knife presses disconcertingly against his spine the moment he pauses, so he steps out into the night without further delay.

Earlier, there'd been a short, sharp shower of rain. Fishmandatu is grateful for the residual scudding cloud cover, concealing his nakedness. Shoved forcefully down the steps of the deck and onto the sand, Fishmandatu notices his attacker steers him with strategic pressure of the knife blade, keeping him close to the tall hibiscus and bougainvillea hedges that mingle with the waist-high sea grass where the perimeter of his bungalow meets the public beach.

They're completely alone. No one to call on for help. No one to witness what might be about to happen here. The only sounds are cicadas and sea.

As the beach shelves sharply away towards the rushing waves, his attacker suddenly charges him again, body impacting between Phillip's shoulder blades, taking him completely by surprise. Hitting the beach hard, he ingests an unwelcome mouthful of cold, wet sand. Rolling over fast, spluttering and spitting, registering the discomfort of sand on his eyelashes, blocking his nostrils, sticking abrasively to his genitals; he nevertheless scoots backwards, crablike, feeling the harsh grit between his buttocks and under his driving heels and palms. The snarling assailant lunges forward with the knife, but misjudges both the speed of Fishmandatu's retreat and the depth of the soft, shifting grains underfoot. He sinks ankle-deep and tumbles forward to hands and knees. The knife flies free, blade briefly flashing in the occasional shafts of moonlight penetrating the shifting cloud. Fishmandatu can't see where the weapon's gone, but at least they're even now. Before his opponent can recover, Fishmandatu dishes out appropriate retaliation, leaping onto his attacker's back and forcing the body flat onto the sand, arms trapped helplessly beneath the torso. Fishmandatu pushes down with all his superior size and weight, gripping the intruder's neck in a powerful headlock and squeezing with determined aggression. Panic sets in quickly, the figure writhing and struggling as Fishmandatu restricts air with calculating viciousness. He leans his head down close to the intruder's ear, and hisses, "Any clues, Nate, or am I just supposed to guess?"

The thrashing body beneath his goes limp. He eases his hold, but doesn't release Nathan. Has he strangled him, or is it a trick? He suddenly realises his erstwhile friend is crying soundlessly. It crosses Fishmandatu's mind it might still be a ploy, so he doesn't free Nate, but makes the decision to allow him breath enough to communicate if he chooses. At length, Nate manages to gurgle, "What the hell do you think you're doing, man? You're playing with fire and you don't even know...! You'll burn us all, you stupid bastard...you'll burn us all..." Nathan's voice again deteriorates into chest-heaving sobs of such apparent anguish it's all Fishmandatu can do to keep his nerve. He kneels on Nathan's back, grips his head, and tries not to feel sorry for him.

At length, Nate's able to speak again, "My wife! My little girl...my Amanda! What do you think he'll do to them? I could kill you! I could rip you to pieces!"

Fishmandatu plays the hard man, "Oh yeah? Looks like it, Nate. You know what, I could just snap your neck right now and roll you into the sea. Who would know? I presume you're not here on your own passport?"

"Fuck you, man! You haven't got the balls, Fishy."

Incensed – why does everyone think he isn't up to the job; Tammi, Simone, and now Nathan too – Fishmandatu illustrates his resolve with a knee between Nate's shoulder blades and an agonisingly slow backward stretch of his neck, until his former partner croaks for mercy, "Phil, please!"

Fishmandatu's face twists spitefully, relishing a type of power he's never experienced before. He tugs millimetres more, then releases abruptly. Nathan's head rebounds like a pea flicked off a spoon, slamming into the sand. He pops up, liberally-coated, blowing, spitting, and blinking with discomfort, unable to release a hand to rub his skin free of its painfully-abrasive mask.

Fishmandatu growls, "Have you been sent here to kill me, Nate?"

"No, no...to watch you!"

"Watch me?"

"To observe. Surveillance! To listen, man! Your whole place is bugged! I've put mics all over it!"

Fishmandatu's world tilts on its axis like a broken spinning-top. The *calls*!

Nauseous, he hisses, "What happens to this surveillance?"

"It's recorded."

"And where do the recordings go?"

Contempt in Nathan's voice despite the precariousness of his current position, "Where do you think the recordings go, Fishy? Where do you fucking *think*? I held back the recording of you calling Simone. I pretended a glitch. I put my neck on the line; literally! Not for you, but for your family – because I know they're not involved in this, same as mine aren't. He uses that fact against you, Fishy. I tried to warn you, man, but you didn't want to hear it. You thought you knew better. Well, you know what, Fishy, you fucking don't. You don't know a bleedin' thing. See how difficult you make it for me to help you out? You don't appreciate what other people do for you, that's your trouble. You just breeze on through, bloody clueless about everything. If I don't get these recordings back on track, he'll know something's up. Then it's only a matter of time before they come for me. They'll come for you too, you must realise that! They'll take Dee, and Amanda…they'll get Reece and Sim. Your boys, Fishy; your little, innocent boys…and your poor old Mum and Dad. They won't get what's happening, but they'll understand one thing – that it's your fault. Their precious son is completely responsible for all their pain. Can you take it, Fishy? Can you handle that kind of guilt? I don't think you can, mate, because the last time life went south, you fell to pieces; when it wasn't even your fault! This time it will be, though, won't it? This time you'll be utterly to blame for *how* many deaths, Fishy? *How* much pain? Can you handle it? Is it worth all that to get your nuts in Rivers and a share of her cash? You realise she hates men, right? So you'll never get to screw her, despite how very much you want to. She isn't like her sister. She despises you. She thinks you're weak – "

"Shut up! Shut up!" The only way to stop Nathan's mouth is to block it, so Fishmandatu pushes him powerfully back into the sand, near-suffocating him for several seconds before yanking him up by his hair and letting Nathan gasp and cough, "What now, Nate? Do *I* have to kill *you*?"

Fatalistically, Nathan croaks, "You might as well. You, me, and everyone we love are as good as dead anyway."

"You're wrong, Nate. My lot are on their way out of the country tomorrow. We can get Dee and Amanda out too, if we move fast! We just have to get a message to them. Call them, and – "

Nathan's body lifts, a monumental upthrust of all his remaining strength and energy, tipping Fishmandatu sideways onto the sand as if an earthquake has begun beneath him. He springs instantly back to a crouch, ready to leap if Nathan goes for him...but all Nate does is flop to a seated position on the sand, groaning, rolling his shoulders and circling his neck. Gingerly wiping the sticky sand from his sore skin, he unzips his right jacket pocket and withdraws a familiar-looking black shape. He waves it casually between them. Phillip's horrified. Since when has Nathan had a *gun*?!

"Point-22. Loud, especially in the middle of the night. Don't make me fire it, Fishy...it'll attract the wrong sort of attention."

"You said you weren't here to kill me."

"I'm not. I told you, I'm here to observe you – to watch, to listen, to record the stupid, naïve mistakes you make every day...only the last few hours, I haven't been doing my job, have I? Like I said, I heard you ring Simone and discuss your half-baked little plan before calling Chadwick and feeding him the bullshit Rivers no doubt instructed you to spout. I'm your mate, Fishy! I held it back. He hasn't heard it yet...but when he does...oh, when he does...!"

"Nate, listen to me – we've got time! Hold the recording back just one more day, and we can call Dee. We can get her and Amanda out! You can leave when I go! We'll all get free together – "

"Chadwick's already asked me more than once whether I'm in on some double-cross with you. I'm not, am I...but he'd already started to question my reliability before I developed coincidental 'technical gremlins'. I've got five hours of time difference to decide which way I go. I either tell him I've fixed it, and I send him what I've got – dumping you and yours well and truly in it – or I bail, and not only is my life forfeit, but my girls' as well. What would you do, Fishy?"

"I'd hold the recording back, Nate – "

"Like hell you would! That's the trouble. I've been a mate to you, but I know damn well you wouldn't be one to me."

"You have to hold the recording back, Nate! I need more time to get everyone out. Dee and Amanda too! You have to!"

"I've got nothing against your family, Fishy. I like 'em. Reece is a smashing lad. The twins are lovely kids. Your Mum and Dad have always been kind to me. It's you I'm starting to realise I've got a problem with."

"What – "

"You're a selfish, spoilt brat, and I think you always have been. I think, deep down, that part of your character has always got under my skin, even when we worked successfully together. Your holier-than-thou attitude; where you are more honourable, cleverer and an all-round superior human being to anyone else who crosses your path, villain or colleague – "

"What's the difference?" scoffs Fishmandatu with bleak sarcasm.

"See what I mean? You're still pompously judging me, and yet you're here working for the same gangster I am! What's noble and upstanding about that? It's squalid, and underhand, and *criminal*! You make bad decision after bad decision, and blame them on everyone else! You married Jonelle even though you weren't that into her…but it's apparently completely her fault your marriage is a hollow shell. How is that fair? You walked out on Simone – "

"She kicked me out!"

"Because you made it quite clear you didn't want to be there! When you had everything a normal person needs for a happy life! You had health, a home, a wife, a child, a stable job, the promise of a long career. Not showbiz enough to satisfy you! You *chose* to screw your mate's missus and get her pregnant. You *chose* to have kids with a woman you knew you didn't love. You *chose* to be here, man, seduced by the money, or the glamour, or – I don't know – perhaps you've just got some self-destructive streak that makes you want to ruin everything good about your life? You had no sympathy for Dee and I when we spent all those years and all that money trying for a baby. You had babies left, right, and centre, and did nothing with any of them! You were too busy casting around for something more exhilarating to keep you entertained! You have no empathy. See why I have trouble with the concept of helping you now, Fishy? Something inside of me thinks you need to learn a lesson for a change. I helped you this afternoon out of habit – some inbuilt sensation of loyalty – but for what? You breeze through life and do what you want, and I'm the shit-shoveller, the arse-coverer; the joker while you're the golden boy. You don't realise all that other people do for you, Fishy. You don't deserve to have help, you won't take advice, you obviously need to learn the hard way; so watch out, here it comes."

Nathan pauses, eases back the cuff of his jacket, looks at the luminous dial of his watch, "You've got four hours, Fishy. In four hours, I will be 'waking up', realising I've fixed my little technical problem, reporting in to our very dangerous boss, and hoping I haven't left it too late to save my wife and daughter from his wrath. I trust that's sufficient warning for you? Four hours to ensure you tie up any loose ends and get your family to safety? My final gift of friendship to you. After that, you're on your own."

Petrified; desperate; Fishmandatu's on his knees in the sand, begging, "Nate, please! Four hours isn't long enough! I just need a bit more time! We can get everyone out, Nate! You, me, Dee, Amanda – "

Unmoved, Nathan simply says, "Fishy, stop grovelling and start moving. Time's ticking."

When Fishmandatu doesn't react immediately to his instruction, Nathan queries sarcastically, "Fishy, what *are* you waiting for?"

Fishmandatu shakes his head, bewildered and distressed, unwilling to abandon the conviction that if he persists, Nathan will eventually cave in.

When Phillip still shows no sign of moving, Nathan extends his arm, and points the pistol directly at his former friend's face, "Four hours, Fishy. *Run!*"

TWELVE

"Dionne?"

"Who's calling?"

"It's Simone...Fishmandatu..."

"Sim! Long time no speak! How are you?"

"I'm...ok... I'm sorry to call so early."

"Doesn't matter. Are you all right?"

"I...am all right, yeah...yeah...um, how are you guys?"

"We're fine; fine. Nathan's away working at the moment. Amanda's got about three months left at Uni and then she's all finished. She's thinking about job applications and everything."

"Wow, already?"

"Scary, huh? Where does the time go?"

"Tell me about it! Er...Dee...did you say Nathan's working away?"

"Yeah. He gets these jobs now and again – bit of a wages boost to do some extra work, and he says it'll look good on his record if he ever fancies going for a promotion."

"Dee, where's he working?"

"I don't actually know. These jobs are always a bit hush-hush...but I do know the jammy sod's in the Caribbean somewhere! I think it's something to do with investigating tax evasion...you know, all these millionaires with their money stashed offshore..."

"Phil's in the Caribbean too."

"No way! On holiday?"

"I don't think so, Dee, do you?"

"Wow…Nate never said Phil was in this special unit with him."

"No, well, initially Phil never mentioned Nate being there either, but it's rather too much of a coincidence, don't you think?"

"Yes, absolutely! Sim, I thought Phil was well out of all that stuff, because of the breakdown and everything."

"Apparently not… Look, has Nathan been in touch about anything over the past couple of days?"

"No. He never gets in touch when he's on an assignment. Well, very rarely…and I get the impression when he does ring, he's not really supposed to."

"Ok. Dee, don't be offended by this, but I know some stuff about Nate that you're clearly not aware of."

The pleasant voice hardens, "Why do you know things about my husband that I don't?"

"Oh God, Dee, I've been trying to figure out how much to tell you. They are *definitely* in the Caribbean; they're *definitely* together, and they're definitely in a *lot* of trouble."

"What do you mean?"

"Phil and I don't speak much normally, so I don't know what he gets up to. I'd rather not know, to be honest. Then, a couple of months ago, Reece started saying he couldn't get hold of him, that he left messages and Phil never got back to him. It's uncharacteristic of Phil. Usually he and Reece message a lot; they have a lot of banter going over text and stuff. Total silence is not Phil at all. It started to annoy me the longer it went on because it was upsetting Reece. He thought it was something he'd done. I just automatically assumed Phil had picked himself up a new girlfriend and gone off the radar…but even then, he'd never not reply to Reece's messages. Then, out of the blue, Phil rang me and dropped a horrendous bombshell that affects us all! He said he was working…for…for…Jimmy Chadwick."

"No!"

"You know the name, right?"

"Yeah, I know it…but…but…Chadwick's a crook, right? Phil was *Police*, Sim…!"

"I don't think any of it is as clear-cut as goodies and baddies, Dee. Not in this case, anyway. Whatever he's doing; whyever he's there, Phil just said it had gone spectacularly wrong, he was in big trouble…and so were all of us. We needed to get the hell out of England."

"*What?*"

"Yeah. He said he wasn't doing the job Chadwick had employed him for, and it would only be a matter of *hours* before he was found out. He said Chadwick would use us to get to him."

"Oh my God!"

"That's not the worst of it. Early hours of this morning, he rings me again. He says Nate's in on it too – "

"He said *what*?!"

"That his escape plan's collapsing into chaos, and I have to ensure everyone leaves within the next few hours – including you and Amanda…and that I shouldn't take no for an answer."

"Sim…are you saying what I think you're saying?"

"Pack up. Get out. Do it today. Just take what you can carry. Empty your bank accounts, and you and Amanda need to get on the flights I'll book for you. I'll text you the details."

"I can't!"

"You can. You must. The way Phil was talking…! He's scared, Dee! I've never heard him sound so fervent and intense about anything. This is big, serious, inescapable, and I think we're on our own here. I don't think the Police can help us. Seems the boys don't know who it's ok to trust any more. We don't have a choice, Dee! I honestly don't know whether this is some undercover operation or not. Regardless, it's evidently out of control! Phil said he's going to do what he can to get he and Nate out. He said we need to do whatever it takes. Those were his exact words. The others will all be going to the airport shortly. I booked the earliest flights I could get. It's just you, me, and Amanda left at home, and the guys out somewhere in the Caribbean."

"Where?"

"He wouldn't tell me. He kept saying 'best you don't know'. This isn't a game, Dee. This is life and death, I'm certain of it! The way he's talking, I'm not going to risk hanging around here waiting to see if it's true or not. I'm just taking him at his word – "

"Nathan hasn't called me. You'd think if it was that serious – "

"Dee! Phil spoke to me less than an hour ago! That's the middle of the night where they are! He said he'd *just seen* Nathan. They'd *only just* talked and Phil was straight on the 'phone to me – he didn't wait for morning over there! He sounded dreadful, Dee. Desperate; terrified! We Need To Get Out! He made me promise not to take no for an answer from you. Maybe the reason Nate hasn't called is he's not in a position to?"

"Where are we supposed to be going?"

"I'll text you. Just pack. Get to Heathrow. Keep your mobile on you so we can stay in touch. Is Amanda at home?"

"Yeah, still in bed."

"Go and wake her up. Now. Get moving. *Now.*"

"What about the house? I've just had the kitchen redone!"

"Dionne, for fuck's sake! What use is a fancy kitchen when you're *dead*?"

"Oh God, oh God, oh God, oh God…"

"Dionne, listen to me. Get off the 'phone, go and wake Amanda, pack up everything of value you can carry and *Get Out*. Please, Dee. I've never meant anything more in my entire life. Run like Chadwick's already on your tail!"

****

Mrs Dionne Palmer. Usually her telephone conversations are so unspeakably bland he can never manage a whole one; almost as if Nathan's instructed her to be as boring as possible. Perhaps he suspects the household calls are monitored? What other explanation can there be for the fact he never rings home?

Chadwick's sixth sense doesn't fail him. He's suspected this for weeks and, finally, here's his proof. No one can *really* be as hopelessly green as Phillip Fishmandatu's pretending to be. And whenever he criticises Phillip's lack of promised progress, Nathan leaps instinctively to his one-time colleague's defence, though he has everything to lose by doing so. That Phillip and Nathan are working together again seems indisputable. Why, that's the question? Can it simply be to free them both from the oppressive weight of their employer's yoke? Unlikely. Nathan's had years in which to squeal to his erstwhile colleague, but he's always kept his head, and his silence. Chadwick's other theory is more probable, and definitely more alarming: that Rivers has made a secret pact with them both – to leave her well-alone in return for a sizeable payoff that'll finance their getaway. No wonder one wife is suddenly on the 'phone giving the other the hurry-up! Simone Fishmandatu's firm tone implies foreknowledge of an established plan. Phillip's too naïve and mentally broken to devise one; Nathan too cautious. This has come from Rivers. She's turned their heads, and changed their minds. Chadwick sets his jaw. This is *not* happening! Both men are there at *his* significant expense, to do a specific job *for him*! *Not* to please their bloody selves…and *particularly* not to screw him over for Tammi Rivers' benefit! Not today. Not *ever*!

He's given Nathan the benefit of the doubt for too many years, because of his unparalleled usefulness. He's plainly allowed the conniving little copper too much rope. Fittingly, it seems Nathan's finally beginning to strangle himself with it. Trouble is, Jimmy can't shake the disquieting conviction he's somehow also inadvertently tangled in Nathan's noose. It's always a risk dealing with Filth. However tight you think you've bound 'em, you can never be sure they won't wriggle free on a technicality – and they always close ranks when the shit hits the fan. Once a copper, always a copper. When he'd very first encountered Nathan Palmer, perhaps it would have been wiser to kill than co-opt him? At the time, Nathan hadn't been able to stop explaining how very much more useful he'd be alive than dead. What if the many years of dependable service have simply been Nathan amassing his undercover evidence, the net tightening all the time around his oblivious quarry? Fortunately, there's an easy way to persuade Nathan to reassess his priorities. It's twenty-one; raven-haired, brown-eyed, bubbly and intelligent. Amanda Palmer: the apple of her fathers' eye.

Chadwick swiftly tugs on his jacket, and takes three brisk steps from the cloakroom cupboard to the front door. He's just about to open it when a sharp rapping on the knocker makes him start, and snatch his reaching hand back protectively. He presses his eye to the spyhole, to see who's paying him a surprise visit before 9.00am. This address is very secret. Jimmy Chadwick isn't the type to encourage guests; he doesn't live that kind of life. If he wants to talk to somebody, he goes out and finds them.

An unremarkable-looking dark-haired man in a grey suit stands on the landing. The main waits but a moment before knocking again, authoritatively.

"Mr Chadwick, I know you're at home. I'd like to speak to you about your morning paper, sir. Can you open the door please?"

His morning paper? Jimmy presses tighter to the spyhole. The fish-eye lens shows the rest of the landing is deserted. The main downstairs lobby contains a security door released by a fob. Quite apart from anything else, how has this individual gained access? Did one of his idiot neighbours admit him? Once inside, a lift conveys residents and visitors to the luxury riverside apartments; one on each floor of the converted South London warehouse. There's also a staircase for emergencies.   The man appears to be alone, but someone else might be concealed behind the fire door to the stairs; it's impossible to tell.   If he *is* alone, he's not a copper.   They do everything in pairs.

Jimmy takes a risk, leaves the front door, and sprints lightly back down the hall to the kitchen.   He snatches up the folded broadsheet that's delivered with his morning milk, unfurling it to stare dumbfounded into his own seventeen-year-old eyes.   Next to him, in the school sports team photograph splashed right across the front page, stands Geoffrey Stocker-Pickford, his long-time friend and one of his most useful business associates.

THE FRAUD IN THE STONE – 'Excalibur' fund a front for money laundering MP?

A quick skim of the article – highly-suggestive speculation and hearsay that's a whisker from downright libellous – before the insistent rapping on the door resumes.   Is his visitor a journalist?

Paper clutched in his fist, Jimmy surges back to the spyhole.

"Mr Chadwick, the sensible course of action here is to open the door.   I would like to talk to you about your long-term financial association with the Stocker-Pickford brothers."

Jimmy hurriedly reviews the first few pages of the paper.   More pictures: a posed shot of Marcus and Geoffrey, doubtless from their fund portfolio marketing literature; a still from BBC Parliament of Geoffrey asking a question in the House of Commons.   Nothing private.   Nothing from anyone's personal photograph album.   Nothing that would point to an obvious source.

Jimmy plants his eye back on the spyhole. The dark-haired man steps a pace further away from the front door, reaches into his jacket, and withdraws a pistol with an unnaturally-long barrel. He aims it down at the door handle.

"Mr Chadwick, I suggest you open this door, sir…or I will force entry."

Backing away down the hall, discarding the paper carelessly as he goes, Jimmy's calculating frantically. Not police. If he was, he'd have to say so, show his warrant card, and state his name. He couldn't gain entry without permission, and he wouldn't be in possession of a firearm complete with silencer, designed to suppress the volume of any gunshot. The Stocker-Pickfords have influence; *Establishment* influence. Who's the unassuming chap outside his door if he *isn't* bumbling local CID, or a nosey reporter digging for an exclusive on a breaking scandal? Is he the Stocker-Pickford family's hired muscle?

Jimmy Chadwick doesn't wait to find out. He dashes through the spacious apartment to the rear fire-exit, fumbling with his keys to unlock and swing open the access door. As he clatters out onto the external staircase, he hears two shots in rapid succession, and the splitting sound of wood giving way. He doesn't look back, but clangs down the fire escape as fast as he's able, grabbing at the freezing handrails as he skids and slips on the wet metal stairs.

Whatever his private suspicions about the business practices of his old and valued chum, Geoffrey Stocker-Pickford never asks awkward questions, and Jimmy always ensures his friend is generously-compensated for his discretion and tact. Idiot baby brother Marcus just does as he's told. Everybody wins. No one actually *knows* anything. No one. Except…?

Rivers!

What had Fishmandatu said? That Rivers would set him up as a fictitious investor in Excalibur, in order to process the inward flow of cash from her offshore fund without any visible links to Jimmy at all! Chadwick had merely chuckled to himself, and thanked his lucky stars they weren't on Skype, so Fishmandatu couldn't see his smirking face. Phillip couldn't possibly know that Jimmy was one of Excalibur's very first investors, helping the Stocker-Pickford boys float their fund at its inception nearly thirty years before…in return for a tiny favour or two further down the line. Jimmy's put grubby millions into Excalibur, and had tens of millions of freshly-laundered profit back. Neither Nathan nor Phillip have the wit to work this out – it'd never occur to them…! It's not a world which either inhabit. These leaks to the press are cunning; a masterpiece of misdirection. This demonstration of deviousness can only have sprung from one brain. If Rivers has rooted around Excalibur's broom-cupboard looking for a low-risk, snail's pace solution to her threatening Chadwick-problem and discovered *this*, no wonder she's exploiting it!

Are the Stocker-Pickfords blaming *him* for the subsequent revelations? He's forgotten all about his intended house-call to Nathan Palmer's precious family. Dealing with two misbehaving lackeys thousands of miles away is currently the last thing on Jimmy's mind. Unidentified armed men shooting their way into his clandestine home when the ink's barely dry on such explosive newspaper headlines is a far more pressing concern. He needs to talk to Geoffrey Stocker-Pickford – *right now*. Only he can persuade his terrifyingly-omnipotent father, the petrifyingly-powerful Sir Blair, to call off the dogs.

THIRTEEN

The Honourable Geoffrey Stocker-Pickford's assistant, Serena, bursts into the office looking both harassed and invigorated at the same time. Prim, uptight, sober to the point of invisible, Geoff chose her specifically because there was nothing about her to notice, let alone desire. It's safer that way, simultaneously removing any hint of sexual temptation whilst permitting her to glide unobtrusively through the corridors of power, picking up titbits of illuminating gossip like burrs on a hiker's socks. She never normally exhibits any emotion beyond mild vexation. In the six years he's employed her, he's yet to see her smile with genuine pleasure, and he's certainly never heard her laugh. Her uncharacteristically-animated arrival is therefore sufficiently notable for Stocker-Pickford to pause in the note he's writing, and gape at her in amazement as she exclaims breathlessly, "Geoff! Have you seen the *street*?"

Stocker-Pickford frowns. He assumed she was coming in with the usual clutch of morning papers for his perusal. His first thought is 'gory traffic accident', followed by the more alarming 'loony extremist attack', and he cocks his head, listening for tell-tale sirens in the road outside. Exasperated by her vagueness, he snaps, "Don't talk in crossword clues! What *about* the bloody street, woman?"

Cowed by his aggression, already sufficiently worked-up to have some colour in her pallid cheeks for the first time ever, Serena's bottom lip wobbles dangerously. Stocker-Pickford groans inwardly.

The first bit of emotional spark the little blancmange has ever displayed, and it's negative. She's going to cry. He hates it when women do that. He grinds his teeth and averts eye-contact, hoping she'll pull herself together so he won't have to apologise or, worse, comfort her. Mercifully, Serena gets her whimpering under control, and points wordlessly to the office window. Sighing with ill-concealed annoyance, Stocker-Pickford reverses his wheelie-chair across the tiny room, noting with spiteful satisfaction that soppy Serena winces when it clangs into the filing cabinet under the window. Geoff eases upwards cautiously and peeps out. The moment his head appears in the lowest corner of the casement, a huge rush of noise and activity bursts from the loitering crowd of assembled journalists, photographers, and tv crews massed on the path directly below. Baffled, unable to decipher anything from the confused babble of shouting voices, Geoff inches open the window a crack. Such imponderables as 'Are the rumours true?', 'Are you going to resign?', 'Do you think your conduct's ethical?', 'Have you abused your position?' float up the side of the building.

Unnerved, Geoff immediately yanks the window shut again.

"What are they talking about?" Bloody hell; Serena! Still standing just inside the door, mistrust in her muddy-blue eyes, two spots of colour like badly-applied rouge on the otherwise wallpaper-paste paleness of her cheeks.

Geoff shrugs with as much nonchalance as he can manage, stomach churning with dread, "No idea! Must have their wires crossed...misinformed, you know..."

"*All* those people are misinformed? And tv too? Has something *happened*, Geoff?"

"Of course nothing's happened!" growls Geoff, defensively, "Don't be so stupid!" He hasn't read a paper this morning; hasn't even seen a headline, watched Breakfast News, anything! What is this *about*?

"But...but...they're all out there waiting for *you*! I just walked through them all and they were shouting things! You *must* know why."

"Oh, must I?" sneers Geoff, sarcastically. Suddenly, he very much wants her gone. Something tells him he needs to ring his father, immediately. He gestures dismissively towards the tightly-fastened window, "Forget it. Someone's got the wrong end of the stick somewhere along the line...or I've been misquoted...or I've upset somebody and they're getting their own back."

She fidgets uncertainly, skinny fingers on the doorhandle. Geoff elaborates superciliously, "You know how pointlessly petty it can get around here. I'm going places. I'm a recognised threat to people's positions."

Knowing she's been in a matter of minutes, he enquires casually, "Did you get those proposals copied, only I'd like to have them circulated soon-as...?"

A tedious hour of standing before the uncooperative copier down the opposite end of the corridor, ensuring it behaves itself, collates as it's supposed to, staples as instructed, doesn't snarl up or break down...should give him plenty of time for a thorough look at the morning news on the internet, and an uninterrupted, *extremely* private telephone call.

Hesitating, as if caught-out, she replies in a small voice, "No…they're not done yet…I went for my eye test first thing today, remember?"

"Oh yes," Geoff delivers his most-winning smile, "Well, best get on with 'em then, there's a good girl!"

Visibly affronted by the blatant chauvinism, she presses her lips together so firmly they go white, whirls on her sensible heel, and flounces out in a cloud of cloying scent. Geoff puts his office 'phone on 'Do Not Disturb', and reaches for his mobile. He's hurriedly scrolling to his father's private number when there's a light knock on the office door. Not in the mood for another trivial exchange when he has something much more urgent to attend to than the business he's been elected to faithfully conduct, he barks, "What *now*?!"

Instead of another member of staff or a parliamentary colleague, in step two men in cheap suits who occupy the minute area between desk and door with instantly-unsettling confidence, "The Honourable Geoffrey Stocker-Pickford?"

Assuming they're journalists who've talked their way into the hallowed halls without permission, Geoff snarls, "Evidently, as my name is the only one on the door, and there's no room to swing a gerbil in here, let alone share office space with anyone else! And you are?"

With well-rehearsed synchronicity, both produce warrant cards and hold them up in front of him. As unobtrusively as he can manage,

Geoff mutes his mobile 'phone, placing it softly back onto the desk, and sliding it beneath the overhanging cover of his computer monitor. Deciding he should stand to command more authority in this exchange, as he's easily a head taller than both policemen, he's disturbed to discover his jelly legs won't respond to his brain's instructions.

"DS Walker. This is my colleague, DC Whitlow."

Geoff jerks a thumb towards the window, "I'm assuming you've come to disperse the rabble? Can't hear myself think in here with that lot hollering right outside. I've got parliamentary business – "

"No doubt, sir, but I'm afraid it will have to wait."

"Sorry?"

"We need you to accompany us now, sir."

"Accompany you?" squawks Geoff, "Where? For what purpose?"

"To our station, sir. To assist us with our enquiries."

"What enquiries…? You can't just come in here and – "

"Yes we can, sir. You know that."

Geoff swallows, grips the edge of the desk, and tries once again to stand. Why won't his stupid legs do as they're told? He looks down. If he can see them shaking, then so can the policemen! He hurriedly wheels himself closer to his desk, "I'm a busy man, Detectives. You'll appreciate I can't just drop everything and swan off with you at the start of my working day. What would my constituents think? I'm accountable to – "

"I don't want to cuff a serving Member of Parliament, Mr Stocker-Pickford, so I'd rather you cooperate instead of making this difficult."

"Difficult for whom?"

"Well, ultimately for yourself, I'd say, sir... As you mentioned, there is a large gathering of Press outside."

"Yes." Geoff pauses just long enough to think about being spotted in handcuffs by the lurking mob, cameras whirring, and whispers unguardedly, "Oh God...what do I do?"

"Just stand up now, sir. Do you have a jacket?"

Geoff nods towards the coat stand wedged behind the door. With a surprisingly-kindly expression and tone, the older officer suggests, "Well, why don't you put it on, sir, and we'll all just walk downstairs together? No fuss."

Nodding, Geoff wobbles to his feet, staggers across to the door, and makes such a performance of putting on his coat that eventually the younger policeman helps him into it. "Much...appreciated," Geoff struggles out with gruff chagrin.

They all stand uncomfortably close to one another in the cramped doorway. "Ri-ri-right," stutters Geoff, "Um...right..." His whole body's shaking so much he looks as if he's just been dug from a snowdrift by a St Bernard. There's only one way out to the street from this end of the corridor; onto the pavement directly below his window; into the clutches of the baying horde with their microphones, their cameras, their questions, and their terrifying truth. How much do they know, and how on *earth* have they discovered it?

"Good God...I think I'm going to..." Stocker-Pickford's immense frame sways alarmingly, and both policemen spring forward to stop him toppling over, easing him back against the desk.

The Sergeant speaks first, "Are you unwell, sir?"

Geoff takes his time replying. An intense, agonising headache is drilling its way into his temples. He thinks if he opens his mouth he'll instantly be sick on the worn and ancient carpet at his feet. At length he manages to gesture towards the office 'phone, and croak, "I think I'd better just ring my wife…"

As they leave the room a few moments later, one officer in front of him, the other behind, Geoffrey Stocker-Pickford glances up the corridor. Serena stands motionless at the photocopier while it chunters and whirrs beside her, eyes as wide as dinner plates, lips still pressed together in that firm, flat, disapproving line. As the Detective Constable takes hold of his elbow and steers him towards the staircase, Geoff sees the thin lips twitch, and the corners of the mouth upturn into a wide and unexpectedly attractive smile.

On the desk in the deserted office, concealed beneath the computer monitor, Geoff's muted mobile 'phone receives a call. Unanswered, it clicks to message, leaving an information banner across the briefly-illuminated screen: 'One missed call – Jim'.

****

He sprints until his chest aches, then strides when he can run no more. His shirt sticks sweatily to his back. He hails a cab, goes but a mile, disembarks, crosses the street, doubles back, hails another, leaves that well before journey's end, and hops on a passing bus to Waterloo Station. He walks the rest of the way, crossing the fast-flowing river at Westminster Bridge, cautiously approaching the imposing frontage of Portcullis House amid the usual muddle of meandering tourists, and all the while he tries to call Geoff. The 'phone rings out repeatedly, clicks to the mailbox…and Jimmy is too cautious to leave a message. Usually, his old friend rings straight back, and not only because they've got on well since Eton, so very long ago – but because invariably returning Jimmy Chadwick's call is worth Geoff's while. Geoff might be an elected representative of the people, but first and foremost he's a Stocker-Pickford – and they've always got an eye on the main chance. Despite it taking Jimmy well over an hour to do what should have been a twenty minute journey, what with all the paranoid doubling-back designed to confound any attempted pursuit, Geoff still hasn't responded. It's not only uncharacteristic; it's downright disconcerting. Jimmy can see a large gaggle of people gathered on the widest area of pavement outside the modernist bulk of Portcullis House; the gothically-photogenic Houses of Parliament and Big Ben to his left. It crosses his mind they might be protestors. He can see long poles in the air that could be placards. The closer he gets, the more obvious it becomes that the placard-carriers are tv sound men with microphone booms. There are also bulky cameras on tripods. A pushing, shoving crew of press photographers vie for the best pitch right outside the door, while a couple of better-known tv political commentators lurk at the fringes of the group, waiting for something to actually happen before they employ their battle-hardened elbows in the melee. They might be there for someone else, but Jimmy doubts it very much. Fortunately, there's a large crowd of curious tourists watching the horde of impatient hacks, delighted-looking pickpockets weaving profitably between them pretending to be hard-pressed commuters with their passage inconveniently blocked, thus giving them the perfect excuse to brush or barge past their unsuspecting victims. Jimmy snorts derisively at this lower class of crook, turns up his coat collar, circles the periphery of the crush, and tucks himself behind a marble pillar a few metres further down the building. He might be a civil servant taking a ten-minute breath of fresh air, or a casual observer vaguely interested in the events down the street. No one gives him a second glance, despite his teenage face being just as prominently-featured on all today's front pages as that of the Honourable Geoffrey Stocker-Pickford M P.

Nothing happens. Jimmy stands there for five minutes. He tries Geoff again. Again, no answer. He toys with the idea of leaving a message this time, decides it's too risky, and rings off once more. He lights a cigarette, puffs ruminatively, contemplates crossing the street and perching on the wall opposite, in case Geoff looks out of the window and spots him…but there's no saying Geoff's even there.

"I couldn't trouble you for a light, could I?"

Jimmy glances up, already sliding his lighter from his inside jacket pocket, more on his mind than the brief, insignificant inconvenience of giving a light to a stranger. His eyes meet those of a nondescript dark-haired man in a grey suit, who smirks, and says, "Must have mislaid mine south of the river this morning."

Jimmy gasps and takes two involuntary steps back. His half-smoked cigarette drops to the pavement. *How* had the guy followed him here? Desperate, Jimmy lunges instinctively, waving the lighter in the man's face. He recoils from the flame, batting it away with an open palm like a tennis forehand. A couple of passers-by glance their way, but most are transfixed by the potential of the crowd now spreading across the other side of the street to stand beneath Boudicca's statue; staring, nudging, and pointing at the tv crews.

Dislodged from Jimmy's grasp, the lighter skitters away, the sounds of the scuffle obscured by the roar of traffic and the excitable chatter of tens of massed voices. Jimmy shoulder-barges his mystery pursuer, sending him staggering backwards down the shallow steps, scrabbling for balance. This gives Jimmy the vital seconds he needs to get away, pelting full-tilt down Victoria Embankment, not daring to look behind him, scattering oncoming pedestrians in his headlong panic.

FOURTEEN

No response to his opportunistic knock on the door. Fuck it; too late! He stands on the path outside the Palmer's house, glances behind him to check the street's still deserted, and peeks through the front bay window. Slatted shutters on the bottom panes provide a measure of privacy, and prevent him seeing much of the interior. There are personal belongings just visible – ornaments on the Edwardian mantlepiece, a large mirror above the fireplace, the tilted edge of a flat-screen tv on a low unit positioned in the rounded bay. He can't see anything else without climbing up, and that's just too risky in a residential street. Someone'll see him, think he's casing the joint, ring the Old Bill and, given the current Press furore, there's no saying he'll be able to pay the coppers off this time, either.

It's perfectly possible Dionne and Amanda Palmer have taken Simone Fishmandatu exactly at her word, already packed whatever they can carry, and fled. He toys with the idea of breaking-in and searching the place, but what will that tell him except that it's empty? Not only is smashing a pane in the front door almost as blatant as climbing on the bay window-ledge to see in above the shutters, it'll just waste more time he manifestly hasn't got.

He *shouldn't* have allowed himself to be distracted from this morning's original purpose by his undeniably-disturbing breakfast visitor! He *shouldn't* have lost his head and dashed to Westminster in a directionless panic! He should have kept his cool, assessed his most pressing problem, and come straight here before his leverage escaped. Yes, Tammi Rivers has released a troublesome genie from its bottle, but it's nothing the capture of Nathan's family couldn't have reversed, if only he'd got here in time! If Rivers can make this mess for her own selfish ends, the maddening little bitch can also be forced to clean it up again! Coerced into renewed compliance by Jimmy's possession of his wife and daughter, Nathan would have no choice but to remain Jimmy's agent in all things Antiguan.

Chadwick is ashamed to admit he got it so wrong with Phillip Fishmandatu. He'd thought Phillip would understand his pain. He'd been certain Phillip's desire for revenge upon Rivers must equal his own. However, Fishmandatu's recent conduct has proved him disappointingly fickle; feckless. Usually such an accurate predictor of human behaviour, Jimmy's reckoned without Tammi's considerable capacity to *scheme*. As Richard McAllister once manipulated Jimmy for profit and protection, so Tammi Rivers has learnt from her former partner-in-crime, and employed those same skills just as successfully upon the suggestible Phillip. Had the turncoat Fishmandatu subsequently worked on Nathan? Was this simply about money and the freedom to begin again, or had a heartfelt plea from a former friend to Nathan's better nature tipped the balance in Tammi's favour? What had Nathan said to him the other day on the 'phone: 'I have regrets'? At the time, Jimmy had arrogantly brushed that aside, the promise of immense wealth and impatiently-anticipated retribution eclipsing all other concerns. He evidently should have paid more attention. Had that been Nathan's way of warning him their association was approaching its abrupt and irreversible end?

What now? His youthful image is on every front page. It's becoming increasingly clear the stratospherically-dominating Sir Blair Stocker-Pickford blames him for this leak; for potentially ruining precious Geoffrey and all the family's high hopes of a Pickford Prime Minister – for where else could his accomplished armed pursuer have originated if not Sir Blair's stable of thoroughbred intrigue? If Jimmy Chadwick considers himself dominant in his own demesne, his influence is but a single flake of snow in a Svalbard winter compared to Sir Blair Stocker-Pickford's all-encompassing sway. With the Palmer wife and daughter gone, has he lost his final opportunity to get back control of events in Antigua, and with them the chance to deliver up Rivers to Sir Blair in order to clear his own apparently-blackened name? He *must* get Tammi, at all costs. It's the only thing that'll save him.

A flash of inspiration: if not alluring, virginal little Amanda Palmer…then how about dynamic and domineering Simone Fishmandatu instead?

****

Simone lifts the empty suitcase onto her bed, unzips it, and wrinkles her nose at the musty smell of stale, trapped air released as she flaps open the lid. There are still a few grains of sand from last years' beach holiday sprinkled across the black nylon lining. She shrugs, upends the large case with difficulty, and watches the dust trickle onto the bedroom carpet. It doesn't matter. It's likely she'll never hoover this flat again.

She settles the case on the bed, pulls aside the elasticated straps designed to hold the contents in place, turns to her wardrobe, and stands before the open doors, deciding what to take with her to a new life with an old husband.

Two sharp raps on the knocker. Simone doesn't think to put on the security chain before opening the front door of the flat.

One hand across her mouth. The heel of the other connecting with her sternum, propelling her forcefully backwards down the narrow hallway. The intruder kicks firmly at the front door and it swings compliantly and silently shut, sealing with a cushioned click, blocking her only means of escape.

Frantic with terror, belatedly recalling Phil's exhortation to caution in all things, she tries to punch and kick at the man, gouge at his face, rip at his eyes with her fingernails, lift a knee into his groin; anything to give her the chance to scramble past him and get out onto the open concrete walkway beyond the front door.

The punches are swift and brutal. The first, to the left hand side of her face, makes her eye explode in a kaleidoscope of black and red dots, head flying back to smack painfully against the coat-cupboard door and leave her reeling. The second snaps her nose, the sound horrifyingly loud, the pain unlike anything she's ever felt. The instant onrush of hot blood fills her gasping mouth; making her splutter, spit, and retch. The third, to her unprotected stomach, doubles her over. As she lurches forward, sobbing now, struggling to breathe, the coup-de-grâce is a knee driving so hard into her face that her head flies violently backwards, impacting the wall with a booming crack, leaving a crater in the plasterboard. She subsides in an ungainly heap on the hallway lino, limbs bent unnaturally, body eerily still.

Her assailant stands upright in the centre of the hall, head cocked, listening to the silence of the flat, before conducting a speedy reconnoitre of the few small rooms to confirm they're alone. Within seconds, the figure is back in the hallway again, surveying the scene. With a frown of distaste, the attacker notes the smear of blood on the knee of his expensive jeans, striding briskly into the kitchen, fussily washing his hands, soaking the nearby tea towel and dabbing prissily at the stain until he's satisfied it's been removed.

Striding back into the hall, squatting before the unmoving woman – careful to ensure the stream of blood that oozes from her nose does not taint his handmade Italian footwear – Jimmy Chadwick shakes her roughly to rouse her. Nothing. No helpless murmur of pain, no involuntary exhalation of terror, no instinctive protestation of innocence. Stomach tightening with apprehension, Chadwick licks the backs of his fingers and hovers them millimetres from her open mouth. No warm breath chills the saliva on his skin. Consternation mounting, Chadwick impatiently feels for the pulse he already knows is absent. For God's bloody sake, what's *wrong* with him these days! Can he not handle *anything* right any more? Alive, Simone Fishmandatu had value. Dead, she's no use at all...and she's already starting to stink.

For a moment, he's at a total loss how to proceed. All avenues of enquiry are closed to him! Nathan's family home's already deserted, his wife and daughter responding to Simone's urgent entreaties to escape as fast as they could – and he's just carelessly disposed of his last remaining leverage this side of the Atlantic!

Uncharacteristically rattled, he leaves the flat quickly without a backward glance, closing the door with exaggerated care as if she's only sleeping. The one consolation regarding this deepening quagmire: the inevitable eventual discovery of his ex-wife's body will link incontrovertibly to Phillip Fishmandatu and, thanks to this morning's ill-advised telephone conversation between the two wives, very definitely to Nathan Palmer as well, implicating both men in this suspicious death. There's nothing to tie Jimmy to any of this…except Nathan Palmer's knowledge; his clearly-troubled conscience; his treacherous 'regrets'. If Nathan's dubious loyalty is finally at an end, then he should be swiftly silenced. So, for that matter, must the unreliable Phillip Fishmandatu.

It's becoming increasingly obvious to James Chadwick that if he wants the Tammi-job done properly, he's got to face the ultimate risk of arrest, get out of England by any means available, and deal with her himself.

FIFTEEN

They come for him in broad daylight. He's ready. He's been ready for hours. The glint of sun on the windscreens of two vehicles swinging up the steep forest road is unremarkable in itself. It's the speed of their approach that gives them away. He swings the telescope from Phillip's bungalow to focus on the trucks, watching as they pull up briefly alongside one another, blocking the whole road: four men in two identical SUVs, finalising tactics; all the more frightening for their complete absence of stealth.

He's packed his rucksack, refilled his cannister with fresh water, obsessively checked his money, passport, and gun. Now, all he has to do is tug the external wires free, slam the laptop shut, shove it into the bag, and dash out onto the veranda.

A determined sprint at the chainlink fence behind the swimming pool, an ungainly scramble up criss-cross steel and trailing creeper, a suicidal roll over the top, and a tumble of several feet to land uncomfortably on his side on the dusty forest floor. A moment to catch his breath and ascertain he's still in one piece, before he's up and off, stumbling through dense undergrowth with as much urgency as absolute silence permits; hoping his unwelcome visitors put the flock of wheeling, flapping, squawking parrots he's disturbed down to the brake-screeching, tyre-squealing drama of their arrival. He'd told Fishy he'd send the missing audio files to Chadwick at first light...but stupid Fishy had done something Nathan had not accounted for. He'd run straight up the beach from their brutal encounter, snatched up his hotel 'phone, called his ex-wife, and instructed her to ring Dionne...on the home telephone line Nathan Palmer knew very well was monitored. He *should* have explained this, but Fishy's attitude stank so much Nathan could hardly stand to talk to him any more. He'd therefore been forced to sit in the villa, four thousand miles away from his only two reasons for living, and listen, helpless with horror, as Phillip Fishmandatu's pig-headedness as good as killed them all.

****

The dead of moonless night on the River Thames, water oily black. Way out East, past the shimmering towers of Docklands and the flashing lights of City Airport, where the river turns and meanders at Creekmouth, winding and widening towards Essex and the opening of the Estuary, a dark-clad figure – slim, tall, lithe, and graceful as a dancer – slips four large holdalls into the cabin of a small, neglected-looking vessel moored to a barely-visited jetty. A few dilapidated houseboats hug the bank alongside, but they are in darkness, their inhabitants safely asleep, leaving no one to witness this solitary departure. The starting of the engine seems loud in the silence, but it's a brief bark soon muffled by the enveloping mist and lapping, slapping tidal water. The boat floats free on the current, guttering in a slow turn away from its mooring, straightening its prow due east, and chugging off unobserved towards the open sea.

****

Tammi wanders absently through the marina. She's calm. It's going ok. She's fulfilled her side of the bargain; it's up to

Fishmandatu to do the rest. When he arrives at the agreed meeting point to board his escape flight, he'll hand over the folder. That's their arrangement. She's confident he'll comply. She's made it quite clear she'll disclose his family's location to Chadwick if he doesn't. It's an uneasy alliance, but one that's in both their interests to maintain.

The warm Caribbean breeze catches at a newspaper abandoned on a bar table right next to the walkway. Pages flapping in her peripheral vision make her jump, and whirl sharply. It's a copy of *The Sun*. An English tabloid on an Antiguan pub table is quite surprising enough, without the accompanying headline and prominent colour photograph. It's of Geoffrey Stocker-Pickford, Marc's elder brother, white-faced and goggle-eyed, being escorted through a bristling forest of microphones and cameras by two unmistakeable plain-clothed policemen. They couldn't be anything else, in their shabby jackets, with their cheap watches and their hard eyes.

MP ON THE MAKE! screams the headline. Tammi looks left and right, before snatching up the paper. Good God...*all* her speculation, supposition, suggestion...but so much *more* she hadn't foreseen! Fleet Street's delved where she was unable, crowbarring open Pandora's Box with their characteristic sensationalist insensitivity. Shoving the paper under her arm, she sprints up the road to the villa, arriving breathless and running with sweat.

Thankfully, there's no sign of Marc. She opens the paper on the kitchen counter, clammy palms smudging the print, and consumes its content voraciously. She didn't ring *The Sun*, so the story's spread already.   That's good.   What she'd intended was a few uncomfortable questions and some unwelcome press attention for the Excalibur investor James Chadwick, in the hope he's the same man responsible for her present predicament. The links and coincidences are myriad and convincing; they've certainly caused this newspaper to draw the same conclusions – that reportedly well-spoken and urbane gangster Jimmy and high-flying money-man James are one and the same. However, far from being bothered about ten-a-penny bent coppers and organised crime, this paper's latched onto the eminently more scandalworthy reference to the illegal manipulation of court proceedings by high-profile figures whose behaviour should supposedly be beyond reproach. Press scrutiny of publicly-available records substantiate her long-held conviction that the Stocker-Pickford boys have been cleaning up the grubby cash of upper class n'er-do-wells for decades.   She's delighted her lightly-sprinkled seeds of doubt have borne such delectable fruit so swiftly. Tammi quickly checks the date on the paper – a day old. It must have flown here yesterday in the hand-luggage of a British tourist. There's still a chance Marc doesn't know. The fact he's implicated shouldn't change their onward plans. Their flights out of Antigua are booked for early this evening. Their new passports are ready and waiting for collection. All that's left to do is meet Fishmandatu at the agreed rendezvous, and collect the damaging dossier. There's clearly a lot more drama unfolding in England than she'd either imagined or intended – and it's evidently now very definitely out of her control; not that it matters. Even if James and Jimmy Chadwick *are* two separate men, both should be receiving sufficient scrutiny from press, and possibly the authorities too, to ensure the dangerous one won't have leisure for pursuit of either her or Phillip Fishmandatu. Plus, any irritation caused to the Stocker-Pickfords cheers her immensely. It serves them right for the obscene way they've always treated her. It's only a matter of time before Geoffrey rats on his good-natured baby brother to save his own self-serving neck. If only she wasn't so necessarily tied to Marc, she could permanently sever the connection between herself and the Stocker-Pickfords...but Marc needs protecting, and it's her job to do it. It always has been. Without him, she's got nothing. They both know it.

Tammi rips the newspaper into long strips, wets them under the tap, squidges the pulp together in her fists, and squashes the soggy and illegible mass into the kitchen bin, concealing it beneath the remains of a chicken carcass. She stands in the silent space for a few moments, thinking...then dashes to the bedroom, fumbles a small waterproof backpack from a wardrobe, fills it haphazardly with a few basics of clothing and toiletries – and makes sure to include her dead sister's passport and a reasonable wadge of cash from the stacks piled in the safe. It's just as well to be prepared...

She trots out to the deck, whips off her sundress, and lowers herself into the cold pool by acclimatising inches, holding the bag high. She sashays down to the opposite end, the water deepening until she's forced to bounce from foot to foot like a moonwalking astronaut; the bag balanced on the top of her head, and her diminutive form submerging each time to nostril depth.

At the infinity-edge of the pool, she kicks her little legs and surges upward, high enough to hook her elbows over the side. The pool is constructed of abrasive composite that scratches uncomfortably against the delicate skin of her underarms and bare breasts. Struggling the bag strap awkwardly over her forearm, she grunts and strains to lift her body further out of the water until she's pivoted by her pelvis on the side, tilting her upper body downwards. Her left hand grips the pool's narrow edge until her fingers ache and daggers of pain shoot up her thin wrist. She extends her right arm straight. The bag slithers down her wet skin from elbow to wrist, wrist to knuckles, knuckles to fingertips; dangling towards the concealed path she can't see but now knows is there. She listens anxiously for the scrape of canvas bag hitting dusty rock. That's it! Safely down, in case she needs it in an emergency. She's never intending to travel on Annelisse's passport again – not when the two brand new ones she requested are waiting in a beach locker the other side of the island – but Tammi's lived too long and complicated an existence not to always have a Plan B, however rough and ready.

She's withdrawing her reaching arm, easing up, about to lower her body back into the water, when a voice behind her demands, "Tammi, what the *hell* are you doing?"

SIXTEEN

Tammi yelps and falls backwards, plunging under the water and scraping her coccyx painfully on the bottom of the pool. She surfaces, gasping, rubbing her injury with one hand and impatiently pushing the thick curtain of wet hair off her face with the other, "Owww! Marc! You made me jump!"

He regards her suspiciously through hooded eyes. An unlit joint hangs from the corner of his mouth. She wonders how long he's been standing there. He sways gently. Drunk. Always drunk. Revulsion washes over her. God, he's vile – how had she ever wanted to marry him? Her conscience pricks, and she blushes involuntarily, *'He wasn't always like this, and you know it. He's hiding from the past, same as you are. He just isn't very good at it – because he feels things, and you don't.'*

"What *are* you doing hanging over the cliff in just your knickers?"

"Ummmm….I thought…there was a crack! A leak! I just had to check it…put my mind at rest…"

"And it was so life-and-death-urgent you had to do it in your pants?"

Tammi skilfully avoids answering this question by countering with similarly-sarcastic passive aggression, "As I have no way of knowing when, or if, you're ever coming home, I have to do all these macho maintenance things myself. Incidentally, where *have* you been since yesterday afternoon?"

Apprehensively, she wonders whether Geoff's somehow been in touch. Surely not even Marc is foolish enough to give Geoff a traceable telephone number that anyone could discover? None of his family are supposed to know exactly where they are. What if he hasn't been sticking to this rule? What if he's been conniving behind her back for the past twenty-four hours with his two-faced brother and lethal father?

He gestures vaguely with his lighter, "Poker! The big game? I did tell you. St John's; remember?"

She swims to the steps and starts to climb out, asking, "Ooh, did you win?"

He smirks, sheepishly, "I…well…I…"

"That was a rhetorical question, Marc. I, and everyone else on this island, already know the answer."

The withering put-down doesn't have the intended effect – to cow him into biddable submission and allow her to pass unmolested. Instead, he stands his ground at the top of the steps, preventing her from entering the house. There's an odd, predatory expression on his face. She suddenly feels vulnerable, naked except for the pair of thin, cotton knickers rendered see-through by their dunking. He's uncharacteristically unmoved by her derision. He just smokes, and looks…and Tammi's suddenly convinced he can see straight through her.

****

A bang…or a boing…or a clunk…or a twang? An artificial sound. A 'forcing' sound. A metallic sound? Phillip Fishmandatu snaps off the shower, and listens intently. There are no other noises. Perhaps he imagined it – his paranoia's certainly ramped up a notch since Nathan's nocturnal visit. It could just be the chambermaid?

No…there's definitely something… A scrape, or a shuffle…? What it sounds like is someone *trying* to be quiet.

He doesn't dry himself, but reaches for the hanging bathrobe, shrugs it on, and eases around the edge of the open bathroom door. He can hear the sea…but took the precaution of closing the doors to the deck before going for his shower; he shouldn't be *able* to hear the sea! With no weapon but the element of surprise, Phillip Fishmandatu makes his decision, tears around the corner, and bursts into the main area of the beach bungalow. The room is deserted, but the deck door stands wide open. Fishmandatu can see a dark-haired white man in a grey suit fleeing across the private beach. He clutches a bundle to his chest, and moves with light-footed grace across the raked sand. Shaken; confused, Fishmandatu nevertheless gives chase – through the door, across the deck, and down the steps into the deep and sinking sand that visibly hadn't troubled his uninvited caller, but which significantly impedes his own pursuit. The fine grains stick claggily and copiously to his wet legs and feet, hampering swift progress, clogging the gaps between his toes until he's hobbling flat-footed like a penguin. By the time he rounds the fence between private and public beach, the dark-haired intruder has vanished.

Fishmandatu slumps against the fence, sweat already surging under the thick bathrobe. Who wears a full suit in ninety-degree heat? He staggers back inside, peeling off the robe as soon as he's able, discarding it on the bed to appreciate the relief of the breeze on his damp skin. He scans the bungalow, searching for a clue, trying to piece together the last five minutes in his distracted mind.

The boing! The clunk! The twang!

He skids across the tiled floor, and around the curve of wall into the alcove housing wardrobe and safe. He stands before its open door, naked and shuddering, the thick coating of drying sand cracking and falling from his lower legs like ancient render from a wall. The lock isn't broken; it hasn't been forced. How had the guy got the door open? His passport's still there, as is the envelope of SIM cards, and his float of EC dollars. What's missing – entrusted to Phillip Fishmandatu on the understanding it will be returned intact or he'll face the consequences – is Jimmy Chadwick's folder!

****

"Commissioner, there's a British Government representative to see you. I've been told his passport and ID check out."

"Who is he?"

"An 'Agent Nightingale', sir. British Intelligence." The aide lowers his voice, and murmurs, "M I 5 to you and me."

"What does he want?"

"Top Secret, sir. For your ears only, apparently."

"Any clues at all?"

"Sorry, Commissioner…no idea."

"He's here now?"

"Yes, sir. He's waiting in the other room."

The Police Commissioner sighs, stands, and plucks his jacket off the back of his chair, shrugging it on unenthusiastically, "I suppose

I'd better see him, then. Organise some cold drinks, would you…and…he's British; some tea?"

The aide grins, and nods, "Yes, sir."

The Commissioner steps around his desk, and stands still at its corner, fingertips resting on the polished wood, "Show him in, please."

"Yes, Commissioner."

During the brief hiatus of muttered conversation in the anteroom, the Police Commissioner whips around to check his faintly-reflected appearance in the framed inauguration portrait hanging above the desk. Tie straight, jacket buttoned, short hair neat…he turns again swiftly at the sound of footsteps. He's standing erect, alert, commanding – every inch the chap in charge – by the time his visitor enters the room.

A tall, slim, dark-haired white man in a slightly-crumpled grey suit. Regular-featured, but lacking any notable characteristics that might inspire further curiosity or suggest the presence of charisma. Not the stereotypical British spy the Commissioner's love of Hollywood movies encouraged him to expect. The M I 5 agent walks forward briskly, extending his hand, smiling politely, and speaking in a bland, clipped British accent, "Commissioner Decker. Thank you for seeing me without prior notice. My name is Agent Nightingale. Here is my identification. I work for the British Government in an investigative capacity."

The Commissioner nods at the ID, smiles, shakes the proffered and surprisingly powerful hand, and indicates the chair opposite his desk. Both men sit.

"Agent Nightingale. What can I do for you?"

From under his arm, Nightingale withdraws a two-day-old English newspaper, unfurls it, and places it on the Commissioner's desk. The front page displays a headline hinting at political corruption, beneath which is a photograph of a harassed-looking man – eyes wide, expression hunted – being guided through a throng of reporters to a waiting car. There's something familiar about his appearance that Commissioner Decker can't place.

Agent Nightingale taps the paper with a thin forefinger, "That gentleman is a serving UK MP called Geoffrey Stocker-Pickford. His father was an MP too, has been Knighted, and sits in the House of Lords. He's a Peer, but he doesn't use his hereditary title. He sticks to the Knighthood...won on merit, or so he'd like everyone to think. Ever since the old man first rose to real prominence in the 1970s, rumours have circulated about the way he does business...but nothing concrete ever comes to light, most of the griping is attributed to sour grapes on the part of those he's leapfrogged to the top, and the guy's stock literally keeps on rising. Today, he's an *incredibly* wealthy, influential, powerful man in British politics and finance. The chap pictured here is the eldest son; a rising star hotly-tipped for a long-awaited promotion to the UK Cabinet in the PM's next reshuffle. Taking into account his father's eminence and the family's pedigree, it would seem his advancement to a high-ranking Government post is assured. However, over the last few days, an increasing number of articles have appeared in the British press concerning his business practices – and particularly alleging abuse of his position to circumvent British law for financial gain; even that he's money-laundering on behalf of organised crime."

The Commissioner picks up the paper, perches his glasses on the end of his nose, and skims the bones of the article, "And this is relevant to me because…?"

"The Hon. Geoffrey Stocker-Pickford has a younger brother. He goes by the name of Marcus. He dropped the 'Stocker' name when he left University and went into the financial side of the family empire rather than politics. It's been alleged Geoffrey Stocker-Pickford is the facilitator, whilst little brother Marcus is the behind-the-scenes brawn. Geoffrey's Establishment connections open the doors, and Marcus's dodgy financial fronts shovel the dirty cash through them as fast as he can."

"And?"

"And…two years ago, Marcus and his wife were on Antigua. I'd like to know if they still are."

"Pickford, you say?" The Commissioner studies Geoffrey's photograph with mounting dread.

"Yes, Commissioner." Nightingale watches him keenly, "You know the name?"

The Commissioner hesitates. From his inside jacket pocket, Nightingale produces a photograph of a smartly-dressed couple at a black-tie party, smiling and posing for the camera. He holds it out to the older man, who twitches visibly upon examining it, and slumps back abruptly in his chair, appearing genuinely flabbergasted. A minute passes, during which the only sound is the breeze rustling letters secured beneath an ornate paperweight in the Commissioner's in-tray, before he asks weakly, "And what exactly do you want with this Mr Pickford, Agent Nightingale?"

"I want to question him concerning these allegations, and determine whether there really is a UK case to answer. I'd like him to, how can I put this…'assist me with my enquiries'…but if he won't willingly do that, I'd welcome his detention by one of your officers, for questioning at a suitable local police station."

"I can't force anyone to comply with a foreign country's investigation, whether my officers detain them or not – "

"Understood, Commissioner…but a nerve-racking afternoon without formal charge in a hot Antiguan holding cell might prove sufficiently persuasive for my purposes."

The Police Commissioner picks up the photograph again and studies it thoughtfully, his expression betraying nothing. Agent Nightingale persists, "Commissioner, this could be press speculation; fabrication…or, the man really could be complicit in international financial fraud! He might be responsible for concealing, or falsely legitimising, the ill-gotten gains of organised crime! If any of the information in this article is true, it could prove highly embarrassing for the United Kingdom Government – "

"I comprehend your argument, Agent Nightingale…but it also places me in a somewhat tricky position."

"How so?"

The Commissioner passes back the photograph as if touching it makes his fingers sting, "I can personally confirm the gentleman you seek is still on the island. However, I must confess a conflict of interest. You see, I know your suspect socially. He's a member of my Yacht Club."

****

Tammi stands at the furthest extreme of the deck, staring across the pool and down to the public beach far below. She can't go and get the binoculars – that'd be too obvious – but…yes, there it is again! A bright flash, like sunlight glancing off glass; the way it had so recently hit Phillip Fishmandatu's own binoculars and betrayed that exact location as his habitual surveillance position. If it *is* Phillip sitting under the overhanging palm trees like he has so many times before – and, realistically, who else could it be – what's he doing there? Is he intending to follow her to this afternoon's specified rendezvous to make sure she shows up? He knows how much she wants that folder – why on earth wouldn't she be there? It crosses her anxious mind he might have outwitted her. But how? And with whom? And what would he gain by doing so? Betray her, and the lives of his whole family are forfeit. He must simply be checking up; making sure. In his shoes, she might very well do the same thing. She needs to remain calm, or Marc will suspect something…and he mustn't, not until they're at the airport and it's too late for him to protest about leaving. Just a few more hours… Stick to the plan, and trust to her carefully-laid groundwork.

The doorbell trills. Still musing on the unproven, yet unavoidably likely presence of Fishmandatu on the beach below, it takes too long for the sound to penetrate her distracted brain. Too late, she decides it would be better not to open the door. Too late, she scurries across the deck, intending to catch Marc before he reaches it, and hiss at

148

him to check the identity of the caller through the spyhole first. Too soon, she sees him depress the handle, and a crack of daylight appear around the opening door.

Expecting the usual Amazon delivery-boy, or one of the neighbours wanting to borrow something, Marc is taken aback to discover four intimidating strangers. The first is a tall, dark-haired white man, dressed in a very un-Caribbean suit and tie, visibly wilting in the tropical humidity. The second is a slim, black man in well-pressed chinos and an open-necked shirt: the epitome of Caribbean cool. The third and fourth are threateningly-large Antiguan constables. As the door opens, this semicircle of officialdom closes in. No one smiles. Unsettled, Marc nevertheless squares his stance, puffs his chest, and enquires, "Can I help you?"

"Mr Marcus Pickford?"

"Who wants to know?"

All produce identifications…but Marc's been here before. He's not about to be tricked twice in one lifetime by a dodgy police ID! Just because they *look* genuine doesn't mean they *are*. He holds his nerve, raises one unconvinced eyebrow, and awaits further explanation. The well-dressed black man speaks again, "My name is Detective Alwyn. This is Officer Craig, and Officer Baptiste." He gestures towards the white man, "This gentleman is a representative of the UK Government. His name is Agent Nightingale – "

A sharp intake of breath behind him. Marc turns in response.

Tammi. In the doorway between sun-drenched deck and shadowy living room; a waif-like silhouette backlit by the dazzling Caribbean sun. Marc glances from her frozen figure to the unremarkable chap in the grey suit who, for his part, is gawping back as if he's seen a ghost! For a fraction of a second, nobody moves. The only sounds are wind and sea. Marc's gaze flicks from dumbstruck Tammi to mesmerised coppers, his sense of foreboding intensifying by the second. Two years…has life caught up with them already? Before he can devise a suitable delaying tactic, the white man acts. Arms outstretched, leaping bodily, he tries to barge past Marc into the villa's hallway. Instinctively convinced by Tammi's reaction that he mustn't admit him, Marc tries just as forcefully to get the front door shut. He's big, but he's unprepared, hungover, and out of condition. He's no match for two fit, young policemen putting their shoulders to the wood. The powerful rebounding swing of the door knocks Marc off-balance and he totters backwards, slamming hard into the hall wall, shocked and winded. The white man thunders past him, easily ripping away Marc's frantically-grabbing fists with startling strength, yelling, "Hold him!"

The black detective does just that, expertly gripping Marc's wrist and shoulder, twisting his arm painfully behind him and propelling him forcefully up the hallway to the living room.

Tammi's gone!

Marc's desperate gaze rakes the room in agitation. Then he spots her, sprinting across the deck towards its low boundary pursued by the lanky British agent. All that's beyond the wall is the cliff edge and the boiling, churning ocean beneath; yet she surefootedly traverses the narrow rim of the pool like a tightrope walker, and scrambles up without hesitation! Her glance back is brief, and not at him. Instead, she locks eyes with her intense pursuer across the rippling surface of the water. The shadow of a mocking smile crosses her face, and she drops…off the wall, and out of sight.

SEVENTEEN

Fishmandatu starts, and fumbles his binoculars. They bounce painfully off his knee and slide down the dune. Swearing, he scrabbles to retrieve them, shaking the sand off frantically, blowing hard on the lenses to clean them without scratching the glass. He could've sworn he just saw Rivers leap off the boundary wall onto the hidden ledge beneath!

By the time he clamps the binoculars back to his eyes and gets the villa into focus, there's no sign of her. Instead, a man in what looks like police uniform is clambering over, either in rescue or pursuit. Fishmandatu spends a couple of seconds observing the cop's rather directionless search of the immediate area, before another movement captures his attention. He tilts the binoculars minutely, and gasps aloud at what he sees.

Above the searching policeman, leaning over the wall as far as he dares, pointing and clearly directing operations, is a dark-haired white man in a light-grey suit!

****

Tammi lands in an awkward crouch and topples forward, grazing both knees painfully and feeling grit dig sharply into her splaying palms. She has no time to examine the injuries. Her prudently-placed 'emergency bag' sits a few feet away on the sandy path. She snatches at the strap and dives into the forest of upright steel piles beneath the pool, leaning back out to scratch and muddle the few footprints she's left in the dust. Just squatting here at the very edge of the overhang and hoping they won't find her is insufficient – that's *Nightingale* up there! No time now to speculate upon whether Fishmandatu's sudden and suspicious appearance on the beach is linked to Nightingale's arrival; or whether this is Marc's fault, maintaining a foolhardy forbidden correspondence with his brother for all this time, enabling Nightingale to divine their location with minimal effort. What she needs to do now is hide, properly. Anything else will have to wait. Already, she can hear the scraping of someone else scaling the wall directly above her.

She scrabbles forward urgently, clambering over the frame supporting the moulded bowl of the swimming pool, stooping first to a crouch, then dropping to hands and knees; finally forced to commando-crawl on her stomach, tugging her bag behind her like an unwilling dog on a lead.

It's hard-going, struggling forward with exploratory fingertips, scared of what she might touch, gripping at the protruding edges of hacked rock and uneven concrete to drag herself on into the blackness. The humid air is close, thick; suffocating. As she gets further in, the space narrows to a slit barely wider than her skinny little body. She can no longer lift her head to check behind her – there isn't room. She's forced to lie completely flat and creep agonisingly sideways like a starfish across a rock; left cheek in the dust, eye winking and watering, body shuddering involuntarily every time a pebble of grit rolls into her ear. In a way, she's glad it's so dark. There are probably spiders the size of kittens under here. She's got to get as far as she can without becoming wedged, because

Nightingale will follow her into the metaphorical fires of Mordor before giving up. She must make this as hard for him as possible.

It's now so tight she's unable to even draw deep breath. She's reduced to panting, high and shallow; the combination of dense, muggy air and hyperventilation rendering her light-headed and panicky. She's almost overwhelmed by the sanity-shredding impulse to slam the back of her head repeatedly against the base of the pool, as if that alone will make the space bigger; to kick her trapped legs; even to suck in enough air to expand her crushed ribcage to its fullest extent. All impossible. Desperate, frantic horror claws at her fragile self-control. She realises she's whimpering aloud, and forces herself to stop. The only effective method of distraction is to keep moving, inching ever-deeper into the unknown.

She suppresses the mouth-drying awareness that, to get out again, she'll have to repeat this whole process backwards, and blind – as there's no room to roll herself over to face the way she's come. Her trembling fingers reach once more, travelling cautiously across a ridge of what feels like crumbling concrete, closing around a raised lip of rock, slithering onward. Her fingers explore again, over the ridge, and…whoa! *Nothing*! An empty space, in which she can wave her arm madly from side to side without hitting anything at all, as if she's stumbled upon a secret cave!

She shuffles forward as far as she's able, shoving her arm into the hole up to her shoulder, circling it; determining, with careful stretching, that there's a space extending at least as far as she can reach above her head, and down to parallel with her knees. Wincing against the compression on her tricep muscle, she angles her arm downwards. Nothing. This side of the concrete ridge, she's squashed almost flat; the other, the ground drops away further than she can reach. She swivels her arm upright. Again, nothing as far as her questing fingers extend. It doesn't really matter what awaits her in there – anything is better than this current, claustrophobic hell.

She inches onwards, thrusting with her toes, squeezing awkwardly past the narrow opening like a bulky parcel through a letterbox. One leg pops successfully into the space and she swings it down, feeling for the floor, heart leaping at the scrape and crunch of her trainer onto the dirt. With slightly-bent knee, she plants her foot firmly, screwing it down hard into the dust, driving through her standing leg, tugging to release her hips and slide her other leg free too. It drops down next to the first and she stands in the cave, folded painfully in half across her ribcage, upper body still jammed in the minute gap. She jerks her bottom backwards, trying to use bodyweight alone to pull herself out – but it doesn't work. Her breasts, by no means buxom, still snag tenderly on the lip of the opening. She's stuck fast!

Grunting, contorting her hands into the narrow space, she pancakes her chest to push past the raised edge of concrete. Shuffling further back, her shoulders edge free without incident, but her head wedges alarmingly. Still on its side, neck pulling excruciatingly, she's reduced to easing it through by millimetres, using her fingers to literally depress and stretch the skin past each obstacle like a baker working dough. The rock scrapes most sharply across her cheekbones. She's so close to being free it's tempting just to yank her head back and hope not to rip anything important off in the process. The whimpering builds behind her nose again. She grits her teeth, exhales, and silences it once more. No point voluntarily going through all this only to betray her position by pathetic nasal whining…but her restraint's at breaking point. One last pull, slicing sharply across her cheekbone – probably drawing blood but she doesn't care; she's out! Relief floods her. She immediately tries to stand in the space, and thwacks the top of her head hard on the pool base an unseen couple of feet above. She swears and totters. Only her firm grip on the strap of the trapped rucksack keeps her upright. Heart thudding, she sinks gingerly to a squat in the total darkness. Ok, so she can't straighten, but it appears she can sit quite comfortably on the dirt floor, and there's sufficient room to fully stretch her legs.

She patiently squishes and tugs the bag through the gap by degrees, much as she'd massaged and coaxed her unwilling body. She then places it carefully on the ground right underneath the hole – the only way she has of marking her original entry point in the complete blackness. If she moves too far and gets confused, at least the bag will indicate a way back out.

No daylight penetrates, but with her cheek against the opening she can feel a vestige of the powerful sea breeze tickling her skin. That's good. If new air can get in, she will at least be able to breathe despite the sauna-like conditions. Perspiration trickles through her hair until it feels as if a million ants crawl on her scalp. Perhaps they do? She can't see one way or another. No. It's moisture in her hair. That's all. She mustn't give head-space to any other notion. She rakes clammy, dusty fingers through her sweat-slick curls, scratching viciously, dispelling the delusion. Her ears strain for information, occasionally catching the muffled murmur of voices and the plonking echoes of feet marching briskly across the decking above. She needs to get her bearings. Endeavouring to crawl straight, she could so easily have veered off on a tangent in the pitch dark.

Thank God she'd elected to leave everything until the last minute, including the packing! It had been for the express purpose of not prematurely arousing Marc's suspicions, but it's now delivering the additional benefit of concealing their intention to flee. She cautiously presses the button on the side of her watch, and focuses on the illuminated dial. She's got to get to the rendezvous point in time to meet Fishmandatu. She *must* obtain that folder! Plus which, the short-hop seaplane she's organised to get him off Antigua and out of immediate danger could now be mighty handy on her own account. If Nightingale's here because of what's in the UK papers, it's certain he won't willingly let go of his high-status prisoner. She can't see an alternative but to leave Marc behind for the time being. She requires a haven from the very real threat Nightingale poses, accurate information as to the full extent of the danger they're in, and sufficient distance to formulate an ongoing strategy accordingly – none of which she can achieve under this kind of pressure. The single, vital decision she must make in haste is how long to remain concealed. Intentional erasure of her footprints will suggest two things to the perceptive Nightingale: either she's abandoned the obvious path and clambered down the rocks instead, hoping to evade his pursuit by leaving no trail; or, she hasn't budged an inch. Will he simply stake out the villa and wait? She shouldn't be allowing this type of thought into her head, but what about water, food, or needing a wee? She should have put more practical survival items in her emergency-bag…but never imagined it would come to this, crouching in the terrifying dark with the threat of certain and complete ruin pacing above her.

If no daylight can get in to the cave, does that mean no artificial light can get out? Is it safe to light up her watch for longer than the briefest flash to ascertain the time? She takes a chance, and illuminates it again, holding up her wrist and using the faint, green light as a torch to explore the space. She runs her fingers along the pool base a couple of feet above her, following it further back into greater gloom, quad muscles protesting at the prolonged squatting. Suddenly, her travelling fingers slide into emptiness! The pool base ends. She can stand fully upright. It's bliss to stretch her body properly, despite the throbbing aches from head to toe. Lighting up her watch again, she reaches her wrist vertically into the darkness and finally understands where she is. Supported by their steel frame, the underside of the pool steps zigzag into the shadows above her. The wall directly in front of her must therefore be the rear foundation of the villa. What she's done is crawl the full length of the pool, and emerge right beneath the patio doors! Unless he brings in a sniffer dog, Nightingale will never find her way back here, but being so effectively entombed is probably compounding her problems, not solving them. If she keeps sweating as she is now, she'll swiftly dehydrate. She has no water, and no way of obtaining any without crawling back out again. All Nightingale has to do is get comfy on the cliff path and wait for her to re-emerge…and that's if she's got the physical strength and mental resilience to repeat the slow torture that delivered her here. Every moment of vacillation brings the rendezvous time closer. None of this has any point if she doesn't get that folder – and a seat on that seaplane to Montserrat is becoming more attractive by the moment.

What to do? To conquer her adversary, she first has to get inside his head. She hasn't removed anything obvious from the villa; Nightingale will hopefully assume she's coming back. He doesn't know about the providential emergency-bag – the thick wadge of cash, Annelisse's passport, the couple of changes of clothes – so once he discovers the cliff path, he'll doubtless park a policeman there to await her reappearance from wherever she's hiding, while he pressures Marc for information Tammi's made absolutely certain the clueless bugger hasn't got. If there's only an Antiguan copper to contend with, might it be worth just wriggling out, chucking her emergency float of cash at him, and making a run for it during the probable hesitation as he contemplates six months' wages fluttering to the dust in front of his nose? But, if it's Nightingale himself lying in wait…? She's not certain he *can* be bought. Well, not with anything she's prepared to offer, anyway.

She illuminates her watch again. Just over three hours, and a lot of ground to cover. How long before it's too late?

****

"Sir!"

"Anything?" Nightingale leans out over the wall, looking down at the lightly-perspiring, sand-spattered face of Officer Baptiste. The broad-chested policeman shakes his head, "Nothing, sir. I've been back and forth along this ledge, trying to get in all the spaces with my torch. There's no one hiding there."

"Remember she's a darn sight smaller than you! She could get in a really little gap."

Baptiste indicates his dusty trousers and grimy shirt-front, "Yes, sir...I did check for that. Got right down, nose to the dirt, shone my torch. There's nothing but rock and builder's rubble. There're some small crevices, all right, but if you got in them, you wouldn't get back out." Baptiste shudders minutely at the very idea of getting trapped in the oppressive darkness. He's not scrabbling around under there for anyone, particularly not this pompous and aloof Brit with his snooty manner and fancy shoes. He isn't volunteering to crawl around getting shit all over him, is he?

"You're certain?"

"I've looked all along, sir."

Nightingale sighs tetchily, "Any footprints, then?"

"Only where she landed – and she's tried to scrub those out."

"So, what, she's grown wings and flown away?"

Officer Baptiste purses his lips, perhaps to suppress a retort he's not permitted to utter, then answers, "Best guess, she's deliberately avoided the path, and gone down over the rocks."

"Really...?" Nightingale surveys the steep suggested route uneasily.

"It's the only other way to get down the cliff."

"Treacherous, though."

"If she was desperate, sir, she might have considered it worth the risk."

"Yes…I suppose she might… What now, Baptiste?"

"I would recommend notifying the Coastguard, in case she is climbing directly down the rocks into the caves right underneath us. There are a lot of old smuggler's tunnels, and hiding places where escaped slaves used to go. Get in there, and she'll be hard to find without offshore access. Regardless, if she has already slipped, you'll need someone to fish the body out before the waves pound it to mush on the rocks." He turns from Nightingale to scan the bluff away to the left, suggesting an alternative, "Of course, she might be going diagonally down the rocks, to pick up this rough access-path somewhere below us. It'd be a less risky route. Still dangerous, but not a near-vertical climb with a sheer drop to open sea."

"And the path comes out where?"

"I assume the public beach you can see way down there. I'm not certain, sir. I never even knew this path was here until today."

Nightingale studies the sparsely-populated expanse of cream sand far beneath them and sighs again, wearily this time. He impatiently tugs off his tie, and undoes his top two shirt buttons, "Christ, it's unremittingly hot, isn't it? Even in the teeth of this wind!"

Baptiste smirks, "It's the Caribbean, sir."

"Yes." Nightingale frowns, and grumpily admits, "I wasn't expecting to have to spend this long in it…and certainly not charging about like a headless chicken. Right, here's what we'll do. Detective Alwyn!"

Alwyn, prudently remaining in the air-conditioned villa until required, strides out onto the sun-baked deck in response to Nightingale's summoning shout, "Success?"

"Not yet. Baptiste thinks she's making her way down the cliffs to the beach. I'm just sending him down this likely path after her." Nightingale points indicatively down the track. Alwyn nods and smiles in response to Baptiste's plaintive glance. Baptiste knows better than to disobey an instruction but, clearly offended by Nightingale's supercilious manner, he glares openly at the British Agent, straightens his hat moodily, and stomps off without another word. Here to get a job done, not to make friends, Nightingale watches the departing policeman expressionlessly until his muscular form disappears from view, before muttering, "Look over the place?"

"Yeah."

"Anything?"

"Laptop. Password protected. A safe…but we don't have a warrant to open it."

"Any sign of missing possessions? Suitcases? Anything indicative of them being about to do a runner?"

"No. Closets full of clothes. Toiletries in the bathroom. No bags or suitcases obviously placed for packing. A quantity of perishable food in the fridge. A normal home on an ordinary day."

They walk briskly across the deck towards the welcome cool of the shaded interior, "And Pickford?"

"Just keeps asking what's going on."

"Oh, *does* he?" Nightingale chuckles, and saunters into the centre of the living room. Mark Pickford is hunched apprehensively on the sofa, the immovable bulk of Officer Craig looming behind him like an Easter Island statue. Nightingale rolls up his tie and shoves it into his jacket pocket, "Where's she gone, sir?"

Marc barks a high-pitched, incredulous laugh, "I don't know, do I? I have no clue what's going on here…and no one will tell me anything! You barge into my house, chase my wife, damn-near dislocate my shoulder…yet *you're* asking *me*?"

Nightingale smiles, and drawls casually, "I think, when we have a little chat shortly, you'll be amazed how much you *do* know…"

He cocks his head at Detective Alwyn, who joins him across the room in the kitchen area. In a low voice, Nightingale instructs, "Right, stick him in the car, and let's get him back to your station. I need to question him at some length. If he refuses to cooperate, arrest him."

Bemused, Alwyn asks, "On what charge?"

"Fraud'll do for now. I also need a warrant to properly search this place, including getting access to that laptop, and a look inside the safe."

Firmly convinced by his dubious manner that the Brit is making this up as he goes along, Detective Alwyn blurts, "Agent Nightingale, you can't get a warrant without grounds – "

"Trust me, I can give you plenty enough meat for a judge to chew on! Come on, we need to call the Coastguard, and pick Baptiste up from the beach on the way. I also want to leave your other boy monitoring this place."

"What?"

"One of those villas higher up the hill. Show his badge, tell the neighbours it's a stakeout, sit his backside on their deck with a decent telescope, and watch this place like a hawk. If nothing's missing, then she's coming back; I'm sure of it…and I'm going to apprehend her when she does."

EIGHTEEN

Agitated by the evident dispatching of the big cop down the cliff path, Fishmandatu stands immediately, paces indecisively, sits abruptly, and fidgets incessantly. Luckily, it's early afternoon – the time when the scorching sun is at its most intense. Everyone close-by who might earlier have observed and noted his erratic behaviour has already left the beach in search of shade. The locals who spent their lunch break lounging on the sand have gone back to work. Fishmandatu's binoculars show the policeman skidding down the steep track, weaving between the rocks and, in some places, having to clamber over boulders that block his route completely. The path certainly isn't a well-trodden ramble. Fishmandatu had been delighted and proud to discover it during his thorough exploration of the villa's surroundings, and saw no other footprints in the dust on his long and tiring upward trudge the day he and Tammi struck their risky bargain. Perhaps he'd been the first to ever use it? There certainly wouldn't have been a reason to struggle up the steep cliffside to the summit of the barren headland before the construction of the Smuggler's Bluff development.

He glances around. Apart from a distant man inflating a paddleboard, the immediate area of beach is completely deserted. The cop's likely to spot him. He'll want to know who he is, if he's seen anything, and what exactly he needs binoculars for in a location where there's literally nothing to look at but flat white sand and endless blue sky. Fishmandatu crawls swiftly around behind the nearest tree. He evidently can't go back to the beach bungalow. Whoever that guy in the grey suit is, he's involved in a senior-looking capacity with the local police…and that doesn't bode well for a fella on the payroll of a gangster. How on earth did the guy find out about the folder? Perhaps someone's got to Chadwick in England? Perhaps the UK authorities already know all about him, about Nathan…about everything! Fishmandatu gives fervent and silent thanks for the morning's lurking misgivings, which providential paranoia caused him to fill his backpack not only with binoculars, water, and a couple of snacks – but changes of clothes, a generous handful of dollars, and his passport.

Now the path's levelling out, the policeman's approaching the deserted beach at a brisk trot. Hidden behind the stumpy palm tree's chunky trunk, Fishmandatu digs a haphazard hole. He takes off his plimsolls and drops them into the bottom. He slides off his t-shirt, wraps the binoculars carefully in the jersey material, zips the whole lot into the bag, and shoves that in on top of his shoes. He uses his forearms to sweep the piled sand back over his possessions, concealing them as effectively as a turtle buries her eggs. He scuttles away at a low crouch from one spreading clump of waist-high seagrass to the next, emerging well past the preparing paddleboarder, sauntering down the beach in his swim shorts, and wading into the cool sea like any other overheating tourist might. By the time the cop rounds the final outcrop of shelving rock and arrives on the deserted sand, Fishmandatu's bobbing head and kicking feet are merely those of an anonymous swimmer, doing gentle backstroke parallel with the shoreline, making steady progress in the opposite direction.

****

It's *so hot*. She's desperate for the drink she hasn't got. She licks the salty sweat off her top lip and tries not to think about sharp and delicious passion-fruit crush over ice; the cool glass opaque with frosted condensation. The sweat that prickled in her hair now runs down the sides of her face, traverses her jawline, and meanders into her cleavage until the nylon bikini band around her ribcage is unpleasantly saturated and sticky. She contemplates removing her t-shirt, but then the dust it's covered in will stick to her clammy skin instead. Woozy from thirst and the increasing build-up of exhaled carbon dioxide in the inadequately-ventilated space, she slumps back against the foundation wall of the villa, and eases down to lie flat on the dirt floor. Drained by anxiety and exertion, she yawns hugely, craving oxygen…needing rest…

She *can't* fall asleep! Her arms feel so heavy she stutters in lifting them to illuminate her watch again. Her window of opportunity is contracting sharply. Despite her exhaustion, she needs to face the long and claustrophobic crawl back out of here, whatever might await her at the other end. She writhes across the earth floor, psychosomatically agitated by the prospect of having to repeat the self-inflicted torment. Exhaling slowly to settle her rapidly-beating heart, she wipes her streaming eyes, and rubs distractedly at a tickling sensation around her left ear, as if someone is blowing playfully into it. Drowsy with the extreme effects of her ongoing ordeal, it takes her a moment to realise what's bothering her is the persistent breath of *fresh air*! Her discomfited fidgeting has manoeuvred her into a position where she can suddenly feel the constant Caribbean wind blowing strongly and steadily!

Cheek against the floor, now indifferent to the dirt coating her damp skin, she edges methodically along the cave wall until...yesssss! Daylight! Not that far away, either! And, clearly visible, the nodding heads of hibiscus blooms in the thick hedge dividing their property from the one next door! How to get to it? Try as she might, the most she can wedge through the newly-discovered low-level gap between floor and steel construction-frame is her desperately-reaching arm up to the obstacle of her shoulder blade. Feet-first is no good either. Her body gets stuck at her hips. There's inches in it. Sliding her legs back into the cave, Tammi the instinctive problem-solver turns her agile brain to this latest challenge. She scratches experimentally at the soil of the cave floor with her fingernails. It feels crumbly enough. Concerted rubbing and scraping does create a demonstrably-deepening dent in the ground beneath the horizontal steel...but, ideally, she needs some sort of implement to break it into chunks she can then scoop away at speed. She removes one shoe and pushes it toe-first into the hole she's created, so she can find the escape route again in the dark. A brief reconnoitre of the immediate area by the dim light of her watch does not reveal a single suitable stone she could employ as a tool...but...! Inspired, she crawls busily back into the lower portion of the cave to retrieve her bag, looping the strap over her wrist and dragging it after her as she sweeps her forearms like windscreen wipers, searching the floor for her strategically-placed shoe. Once rediscovered, she kneels before the hole, and extracts her old wooden hairbrush from the overstuffed pack, careful not to let anything else fall out as she does so. The brush has a sturdy handle which tapers to a sharp point – doubtless intended for styling rather than digging oneself out of a subterranean prison, but Tammi's nothing if not resourceful. She bends again, chin to the dirt, double-checking the position of the slice of daylight, before gripping the brush around the bristles and driving the pointed handle with all her might into the compacted earth. Several determined strikes like a psycho in a B-movie and she pauses, dripping sweat and panting, using the light of her watch to assess her handiwork. It's gone surprisingly well. Way back here where the bulk of the groundwork took place, the earth's more builder's sand and topsoil than billion-year-old bedrock. It's cracked and crumbled with relative ease. She's just got to make the trench a few inches deeper.

The sweat courses off her, dripping from her nose, her chin; running down her arms and plopping off her elbows. It doesn't matter how disgusting she becomes; she's just got to get out. Breathless; shoulders, neck and back burning; pins and needles in her lower legs from having to do all this kneeling down and stooping forward – progress is frustratingly slow; the cycle of chisel, scrabble, scoop proves maddeningly laborious, but the dip enlarges encouragingly with every downward stab…and hope grows…

****

Half a mile down the long, straight beach, lolling in the surf the very image of the carefree tourist, Phillip Fishmandatu struggles to determine what's happening back at the base of the cliff. The paddleboarder's long-gone by the time the policeman finishes his examination of the area at the immediate foot of the jutting headland, and turns his attention to the beach instead. He takes a cursory wander up to the dunes at the back, standing nerve-janglingly close to Fishmandatu's freshly-dug hole. A police Jeep pulls up on the verge a few yards further down the sand. A figure climbs out and trudges to meet the cop. At this distance, and over such an expanse of brightly-glittering water, Fishmandatu can't determine whether it's one of the individuals he'd earlier observed up on the deck of the villa. During their lengthy conference, a Coastguard speedboat zips past outside the line of safe-swimming buoys, the wake from its outboard creating sufficient turbulence to bob Fishmandatu's body around like a cork. He's trying to keep as much of himself below the waterline as possible, making him harder to spot. He'd like to be mistaken for the swell of a wave, or a solitary rock exposed by the tidal ebb. He kicks for shore, driving his fists into the sinking sand to hold position in the shallows, gasping as the accelerated waves from the boat's wake break over his head.

Both figures stride down to the edge of the surf. The Coastguard boat drifts in until it's almost beached, taking the same advantage as Fishmandatu of the sharply-shelving seabed. As far as he can see, animated discussion ensues – plenty of gesticulation up at the cliff and around the headland – before the Coastguard boat's outboard gurgles back to life, the lightweight craft swings effortlessly against the tide, and it picks up speed, skimming over the rolling waves and around the bluff, disappearing from sight. The two men left on the beach mooch back up the sand to the waiting Jeep, which performs an unwieldy five-point-turn on the narrow coast road, and chugs off.

One guy down the hillside. One out of the Jeep. No one out of the Coastguard vessel. No one else out of the vehicle. The two figures on the beach back into the Jeep, and away. That surely means there's no one left to observe the unearthing of his hidden possessions? Should he give it a bit longer?

A glance at his waterproof watch. Given the events of this morning, he'd very much like to be early to the rendezvous point, conceal himself somewhere, and observe Rivers' behaviour – that is, if she shows up at all. Fishmandatu still retains a nagging suspicion she's somehow responsible for the theft of the folder. He'd be completely convinced of her utter duplicity, but for the fact she's honoured every other aspect of their unconventional bargain. She's fronted up money for hotel rooms, booked flights…in fact, done everything she promised to get his family to safety. Why bother, if her intention's been to pinch the folder all along? If the removal of the folder from the safe is nothing whatever to do with Tammi, he mustn't let on he no longer has it – until it's too late for her to refuse to honour the final element of their agreement. Lying in wait at the rendezvous point and choosing the very last moment to emerge might be the best way to wrong-foot her, while he uses the intervening period to invent a brilliant reason why she shouldn't immediately betray him as it appears he's cheated her.

It suddenly strikes Fishmandatu that the theft could be absolutely nothing to do with him, or even Jimmy Chadwick! It occurs to him that in the extremely-precise removal of the folder – and *only* the folder – from the bungalow's safe, he might simply be collateral damage. This could be *all* about Gatwick airport two years ago; about identity theft, and complicity in historical fraud! If Tammi so desperately wants that folder because of the raft of long-term evidence it contains, then so might others. Fishmandatu experiences a sudden rush of optimism. Perhaps his hopeless, fruitless private agony might be relieved after all? Justice might be imminent! The resurrection of his own trashed reputation, and atonement for the undeserved deaths of poor, unlamented Annelisse and their secret, lost baby! Phillip Fishmandatu splashes a haphazard front-crawl back down the shoreline towards his buried stuff, heart soaring despite the exertion. Potentially, the easiest way to destabilise Rivers is simply to tell her the truth and allow her perceptive brain to consider its alarming implications; namely, that someone else now has the folder and the leverage it contains: the mysterious dark-haired intruder in the light-grey suit.

NINETEEN

Agent Nightingale rolls up the sleeves of his increasingly damp and crumpled shirt. It's so hot in this interview room even the gaps between his toes feel slimy with sweat. He's uncomfortable, weary, and exasperated by the lack of predicted progress. By contrast, the man his tactics were originally designed to discomfit seems remarkably unruffled; sanguine, even. Most of Nightingale's questions have been met either with face-scrunching incomprehension or head-shaking bafflement. He's either a superlative performer, or he genuinely hasn't a clue. For all his years of extensive training, and inherent low cunning, Agent Nightingale truly cannot identify which it is. He sighs, drags a hand down his perspiring face, and intones, "For the purposes of my recording, Mr Stocker-Pickford, who is the woman in this photograph?"

Nightingale slides the same picture across the table that he'd earlier shown to Police Commissioner Decker. Marc leans forward, looks, sits back, and answers calmly, "My wife."

"Her name? For the recording."

"Annelisse."

"And the woman who turned tail and ran from your villa this afternoon?"

The slight furrowing of the broad brow as if in confusion, "Um…my wife…?"

"Are you *certain* of that, Mr Stocker-Pickford?"

"I don't really understand your question. Are you saying I don't know my own wife?"

"I'm not saying anything of the kind. If that woman *is* your wife, Mrs Annelisse Stocker-Pickford – "

"Who *else* would she be?"

"Why did she run, sir?"

"I have no idea! Why are you asking me? I have no clue what is going on here!"

"Innocent people don't tend to sprint for cover the minute they see the police – "

"They might if they're scared out of their wits by people *dressed* as police, storming their way into a private property! We've experienced this before! If you'd done your homework, you'd know we were forced to leave the UK because we lost our house to a confidence-trickster *masquerading* as a police officer! I'm still not sure I saw a warrant this afternoon, granting you permission to enter my property…before your boys damn-near took my head off shoulder-barging the door down…?"

"Perhaps if your wife hadn't elected to run, most-suspiciously, and you hadn't violently attempted to refuse us entry, Mr Stocker-Pickford – "

"I prefer just 'Pickford', if it's all the same to you. I dropped the Stocker part of the name a long time ago."

"Yes…and whose idea was that?"

"What?"

"Creates a subtle demarcation between public and private sides of the empire, doesn't it, sir…even when it's exactly the same person pulling both sets of strings? Just that one little change can make the connection so much less obvious…"

"I'm not sure I understand what you're implying – "

"I know who your father is, Mr St-…*Pickford*."

"Bully for you. Can't say I have much to do with him these days."

"Why not?"

"I'm not sure that's any business of yours."

"You brought it up, sir. Thought you had something to get off your chest."

Marc chuckles mirthlessly, and replies, "Can I go now?"

"I'm afraid that won't be immediately possible."

"I'm not under arrest…so you said."

"We need to discover the whereabouts of your missing wife before we can permit you to reenter your property. It's under observation until she returns. Plus, the quicker you begin *answering* my questions instead of avoiding them, the closer you'll be to going home."

"As I keep telling you, I can't give you answers to things I don't know, can I? However many times you ask me! And I've never been much cop at making stuff up; not quick enough on the uptake."

"The rude health of myriad investment funds under your apparent supervision suggests your self-deprecating manner belies considerable 'quickness', Mr Pickford."

"Eh?" Marc's demeanour instantly alters; the abrupt shift from personal to professional unbalancing him more than he's able to conceal. Nightingale smiles nastily, and asks lightly, "Keep up much with the news from home? Follow the UK press at all?"

Pickford clears his suddenly-clogging throat, "Now and again…it's all the same old guff, isn't it?"

"And UK Politics?"

Marc snorts derisively, "Politics? You can keep it! I've had enough of that to last a lifetime."

From the chair next to him, Nightingale lifts a rustling object that reveals itself to be a broadsheet newspaper. He unfolds it, placing it softly on the table before Marc Pickford, purring, "All a bit too close to home, eh?"

The colour drains from Pickford's face as he absorbs the photograph, the headline, the first few paragraphs of explosive revelation. His eventual response comes out as little more than a croak, "If it's all the same to you, I think I've finished 'helping you with your enquiries' now."

Nightingale smirks stiffly, and pauses the recording on his mobile 'phone, "Have it your way, Mr Pickford…but I would strongly urge you to consider what usually results from a decision made in haste. You see, if you've suddenly found yourself 'unable' to help me, I am duty-bound to warn you that there'll correspondingly be very little *I* can do to help *you*."

****

Tammi writhes awkwardly through the upright steel rods that protrude like clumps of bamboo from the concrete foundation pad and coat her already-grimy body in a speckled graffiti of orange rust. She somehow needs to clean herself up before daring to be seen in public. She looks down at the state of her clothing. Even in the gloom she's indescribably filthy, with thick stripes of mud down her legs, grazed knees a mess of embedded grit and congealing blood, arms scratched, dirty, and rust-streaked, hands and nails vile with ingrained earth from digging, and her clothing stained red by sweat-soaked soil. Her cheek feels sore where she probably cut it impatiently tugging her trapped head free of its concrete vice. The quickest way to deal with all this would be to discard her t-shirt, take the path to the beach, sprint straight into the sea before anyone spots her, and wash off as much of it as she can…but that's only possible if there's no reception committee on the cliff ledge awaiting her reappearance.

There've been no sounds from the deck above her for ages. That doesn't necessarily mean she's out of immediate danger; they might be inside the villa, or sitting in wait for her somewhere on the cliff path. That's it, she's finally through the coppices of rusting steel, and out! Exhausted, slumping to one hip under the very edge of the deck, shaded by the reaching branches of the hedge dividing their property from next door, she relishes the simple joy of physical freedom, and luxuriates in strong breeze cooling mucked-coated skin.

Despite her raging thirst, physical exhaustion, and the considerable combined discomfort from her plethora of minor injuries, she creeps forward into the hedge with deliberate care, resisting the impulse to hurry and set the foliage waving to betray her presence. Cocooned protectively within, she crawls the extent of the deck, all the way back to the cliff path. She parts the branches immediately before her, and peeks cautiously out. As far as she can see along the ledge in either direction, there isn't a soul…but a trail of very large shoeprints travels straight past her hiding place, virtually under her nose. The treads on the soles are so clearly-defined, they suggest either that the heavy individual responsible stamped their way down towards the beach with some passion, or that the prints are very fresh, the strong wind lacking sufficient time to blur the distinct edges. A swift dip in the Caribbean Sea is evidently out. If she follows those tracks down the cliff, she'll likely encounter whoever made them; probably an Antiguan copper ticked-off with getting dust on his shiny boots, waiting impatiently to take his annoyance out on the someone who definitely deserves it.

She sinks back into the centre of the hedge, crouching, taking stock. Another glance at her watch. Time is seriously pressing now. She needs to start making some proper progress. She firmly rejects the cliff path, despite it being the easiest escape route. Too risky. She's no idea what's at the bottom. Returning to her property is similarly not an option. Just because Nightingale's being quiet, doesn't mean he isn't still there. Hang on, though! If climbing up onto her *own* deck isn't possible, what about climbing onto someone *else's*?

The villa to her left is the last in their row. Owners Siggi and Rosie are German, only visit four times a year, rent the place out sporadically to friends and family inbetween, and the rest of the time it's empty. Marc and 'Annelisse' Pickford – 'that *lovely* English couple next door' – keep an informal, neighbourly eye on it for them. At the moment, there's no one staying there! She can use the cover of the hedge and trellised privacy-screen to conceal herself from anyone watching in her villa, get onto Siggi and Rosie's deck as quietly as possible, have a *drink* – a wonderful, incredible, necessary, blissfully-cold drink – from their outdoor bar…even give herself a cursory wash! From Siggi & Rosie's, she can drop over the far wall into the narrow access-alley that runs front-to-back between their place and the retaining wall of the development. It's the best chance she's got of getting out of here unobserved! She vaguely recalls a gate at the end of the alley, but struggles to accurately picture it, kicking herself for not being more observant. It is high? Barred? Wooden? Locked? It's immaterial, really; she *must* make the rendezvous point in time to meet Fishmandatu, or he'll get on the bloody plane *she's* paid for, and take her folder with him! She hasn't any time to waste. She's just *got* to make this work, whatever the obstacles. Surely, after everything else she's already experienced this afternoon, getting under; through; or over a gate of any sort will be child's play in comparison? It crosses her mind Nightingale could have planted a cop on the empty deck next door…or a waiting chorus-line of them out the front to nab her as she scales the gate – but instinct tells her he's concentrating on the back of the villas. That's what she'd do. There are motion-activated CCTV cameras mounted on the development's main gate. No fugitive in their right mind would stroll straight out the front in broad daylight, cross a communal car park where anyone could see them, and leave via the grand, camera-monitored entrance…so that's exactly what she's going to do. She won't know whether there's a copper on next-door's deck until she climbs up there – and the time for caution is long past; she's just got to *do* this! Tammi slides her rucksack onto her back, creeps deeper into the dense hibiscus hedge, and starts to climb.

****

Fishmandatu gets the taxi driver to drop him at a roadside café. He buys an ice-cream and wanders casually along the side of the highway. A few hundred metres down the road, he surreptitiously checks he's unobserved before ducking into the rainforest and working his way diagonally towards the off-road trail he needs to follow to the rendezvous point. Down on the forest floor amongst the densest undergrowth, not a breath of welcome wind alleviates the intense afternoon humidity, making progress slow and enervating. He'd never have considered a daytime escape, but Rivers' plan is ingenious in its simplicity. Attempt to slip away under cover of darkness, and there'll always be someone around who'll spot the unusual nocturnal activity; notice a light where one never shines, a car where vehicles shouldn't drive, foreign voices they don't recognise. In the daytime, who'll look twice at another light plane of day-tripping island-hoppers?

He stops for a breather, peering ahead up the shady trail. He can see a narrow path snaking off to the right. That must be the one. A matter of fifteen strides down the sandy track and he emerges onto a secluded beach. To the far left-hand side, a rickety wooden staircase climbs up to a derelict, hurricane-decimated villa perched on an outcrop facing the sea. Now, *that* would be an exclusive address. What a location! Private beach, ringed by rainforest on three sides – a smuggler's paradise! Fishmandatu stops short on the sand, and grins ruefully. His moral compass has shifted dangerously these last few months, almost without him being aware of it. Before he sees his family again, he must realign his values; get himself back on the right track. He isn't yet quite ready to completely surrender the soul of the true Phillip Fishmandatu to utter iniquity. In his humble opinion, there's still something about the geezer that's worth fighting for.

To his right is a dilapidated pontoon that juts from the beach into the gently-rolling waves. The legs that by some miracle still support it are black with age, coated in crustaceans, and thick with trails of weed that wind and curl with the motion of the water. Metal struts and screws show here and there, burnt-orange with rust in the slimy shadows beneath the structure. By contrast, the remaining planks of the broken walkway are bleached silver by sun exposure.

He's nice and early. He wanders along the treeline, searching for a suitable place to hole-up and await Rivers' arrival. Settling on the shade-dappled sand with an unobstructed view of the pontoon and beach, a sun-warmed fallen tree at his back; Phillip slouches in unexpected contentment. He's even enjoying the tight, sticky sensation of the dry sea-salt still coating his skin – confidence-boosting proof of the earlier escapade successfully survived. He'll get to his Montserrat hotel, wash off the grime of his adventures, confirm his own onward flight, and be out of the Caribbean before dinner-time, never to return. He just has to confound Rivers long enough to get on the rescue plane. Apprehension churns his empty stomach, diluting the complacency that's been sustaining him since lunchtime. He can't yet relax, can he? So far, Tammi Rivers has proved unpredictable; indomitable. Outwitting her for long enough to clamber aboard a seaplane and refuse to disembark, despite the fact he's reneged on his part of their bargain, might be a challenge too far. For example, he has no idea who'll be flying the thing! Will it be a mercenary employed to do Rivers' bidding, whatever that might be?

He's encouraged by the notion that although circumstances have changed for him since this morning, they might well have taken an equally-detrimental downturn for Tammi too. If the dark-haired man is indeed a British investigator of some sort; if he's specifically tracked down and removed the folder from Fishmandatu's possession for the prosecutorial evidence it contains against her, then whether Phillip goes or stays is surely the least of her worries? He's been making baseless accusations against she and Marc Pickford for two years, and where's it got him? With no evidence, and no credible support – not even from his family – he's had no proof and no case. Losing the folder, he reverts to what he's been ever since that terrible night at Gatwick: a toothless irritation. The world considers him crazy. Only he, Tammi, Marc, and Jimmy Chadwick know he isn't. If he points this out…if he *pleads*…? Outwardly, she may intimidate, deride, scheme, and manipulate…but her *actions* prove her sufficiently compassionate for Fishmandatu to be persuaded of arousing her pity at the very least. If he throws himself upon her mercy, given he no longer retains any means to do her harm, might she relent, and just let him join the family she's been instrumental in rescuing? None of this is for his benefit, after all; the whole plan's been devised to gain possession of the folder and secure his future silence…but she's still done something benevolent for a group of innocent strangers she'll never meet, and from whose survival she'll never directly profit. Somewhere behind that impenetrable exterior lurks a heart, and a conscience; Phillip Fishmandatu is sure of it. What *is* it about the Rivers twins; both able to dominate and direct him with capricious abandon at the expense of his bedraggled dignity, when no other women have ever come remotely close to troubling his conceited self-absorption – not even his wives!

Just over an hour to wait for the plane. He fumbles a packet of peanuts from his bag and munches them unhurriedly, probing tongue chasing lumps of nut from between his teeth. His hooded eyes lazily watch the hypnotic swell of the tide up and down the supporting beams of the old pontoon. Will Rivers show? He sips his water sparingly, and conserves his energy for what's shaping up to be the literal fight of his life…surprised by quite how much he desires this battle.

TWENTY

Tammi's climb is careful; gingerly easing through gaps in the branches, holding them taut and releasing them gently as she passes, desperate not to give herself away. Eventually, she reaches the level of the trellis, around which twists tendrils of passion fruit to provide an impenetrable screen of greenery between each property; meaning, of course, that she can't see clearly onto either deck. She reaches out, grips the wall a couple of feet above her, hooks a foot, a knee, a thigh, finally breaking cover and throwing herself over in a fully-committed sideways roll intended to expose her to any observation for the shortest-possible period. She finishes flat on her back on Siggi and Rosie's deck, winded and amazed, staring up at blue sky, dazzling sun, and wheeling sea birds. She lifts her head and looks around. The deck is empty. The roller shutters on the doors and windows are closed. She's alone here! If she keeps her head down and sticks close in the cover of the building, she can get right across the deck and repeat the same process, rolling over the far wall and into the access-alleyway beyond.

She tries crawling on all-fours, but her skinned knees sting so much she has to wriggle on her stomach instead. She struggles clumsily past the villa's shuttered patio doors, and around into the outdoor kitchen on the opposite side of the deck. She leans up against the cupboards, heart hammering with toil and terror. Directly above her head is the sink…she needs a drink *so much*.

Easing cautiously upwards, exhausted quad and glute muscles burning with the tension, she reaches an arm across the worksurface and snaps on the lever tap. She ducks down into cover again. The tap seems deafening, gushing into the metal sink at full pressure. Nothing happens. No shouts from next door; no running feet in response to the running water.

She can't wait any longer. Popping her head back up, chin on the cold edge of the sink, she scoops desperate handfuls of delicious refreshment into her gasping mouth. What she can't imbibe fast enough pours down her front, drenching her t-shirt, shockingly icy against her hot body. At first, she gulps and gulps as if she'll never swallow enough to satisfy her thirst…but gradually the initial fever abates. Her swollen tongue no longer sticks to the roof of her mouth. Her sensitive teeth tingle with abrupt awareness of the cold. She stops drinking, belches, and smacks her lips, grimacing at the granular taste of mixed mud and sweat coating them like foul lipstick. She wets her hand again, rubbing it around her face, drawing in sharp breath as her dirt-roughened palm scratches across her tender cheekbone.

Snapping off the tap, she flops back to a seated position and peels off her vile t-shirt, turning it inside-out and using the soft, soaked material to dab gently at her face. Spots of blood show on the grubby white jersey. Her cheek is definitely cut; how badly, she has no idea. She tries to use the shirt to wipe some of the sticky soil off her arms and legs – but it only smears and spreads the stripes of grime onto the cleaner bits. A waste of time; she discards the t-shirt on the floor. She opens and shuts the cupboards closest to her, but they're all empty. There's nothing suitable that'll function as a drink container, so she'll have to get used to thirst again before long. Tempting though it is to sit hidden here – lulled into a false sense of security by the cosiness of the tiny galley kitchen under the shade of its banana-thatched roof, and comforted by the knowledge of water within easy reach – rest is not an option. The plane will be at the deserted beach pontoon in a couple of hours, and she's got two new passports to collect on the way.

Reluctantly, Tammi abandons her latest refuge and scuttles to the end of the kitchen, peering cautiously around the edge of a cupboard. This is the first element of her escape plan she can't execute under cover of hedges, walls, or buildings. There are no handily-placed obstructions in the few feet between the end of the kitchen and the nearest scaleable section of boundary. She can't see anyone on her deck, or on those of the villas beyond it. There's no moment better than the next. If the deck's under observation, she'll be seen whether she goes for it now or waits ten nervous minutes for nothing.

Tammi tugs at the straps of her compact black backpack. She needs it to sit close to her body and move with her. She doesn't want anything flopping around getting caught or attracting extra attention. Rocking forward to a crouch, balancing on the balls of her feet, she springs out into the open, taking two fully-extended leaps and flinging herself bodily over the wall without pause for preparation.

****

Stationed on the rear deck of a bungalow higher up the hillside, slouched in a rattan chair, Officer Craig lazily scans the area around the Pickford villa through the old binoculars from the police car's glove compartment. He's already eaten several biscuits from the mounded plate at his elbow, drunk a tall, sugared glass of iced tea from the jug that stands beside it, and watched the overweight husband-of-the-house drag a heavy patio umbrella across the deck to provide him shade under which to conduct his observation. All very amusing…especially as he's of the opinion his stakeout's pointless. However, if an English Government Agent wants him to look at the scenery until the end of his shift – and his superiors agree – who is he to argue? Someone's meant to be coming from base with a decent telescope on a tripod, but they're clearly also dragging out their own assignment; probably driving the long way with the radio playing and the windows down. Who can blame them? If he'd been given that particular task on such a muggy day as this, he'd be milking it too. The binoculars are sufficient, anyway. He doesn't need a flashy telescope to watch nothing happen.

He reaches to pop in another whole cookie, masticating unattractively, rolling his shoulders and pretending to thoroughly scan the area beneath his vantage point…when in fact he's allowing his eyes to glaze, stifling a biscuity yawn, and wondering idly whether there'll be any overtime in this…oh! What was that? A movement? A round, dark shape hopping onto a distant wall, and disappearing just as quickly down the other side. A cat? And which wall? He hadn't really been looking properly. It was close to the Pickford property, for sure…but actually on their deck itself? He squints through the binoculars. The property looks deserted. So do those on either side. It must have been a cat. A small, round, black shape. What else could it have been? If they'd been in his neighbourhood, he'd have assumed it was a chicken, but no one keeps chickens at swanky Smuggler's Bluff!

Officer Craig moves the binoculars with purpose now – up and down in a grid pattern, trying to take in every square foot of immediate area surrounding the Pickford villa – suddenly longing for the focusing power of the absent telescope. If he's missed a vital clue whilst shoving fig rolls in his face, the undeniably-menacing Nightingale will have his badge for making a mockery of an international investigation. Reluctant though he is to leave his peachy perch, Officer Craig knows he's got to get down there and have a thorough look. He abandons his binoculars on the table, brushes the considerable quantity of crumbs off his neatly-pressed trousers, and sprints for the door.

****

It's only as Tammi rolls over the wall she realises the drop is far bigger on this side than on the other, and there's no trellis to grab on to; no foliage to land in to break her fall. She flexes her toes frantically, digging her plimsolls into the rough render in a bid to create some friction to slow her tumble. She reaches up desperately, left hand unbelievably getting purchase on the top of the wall! It succeeds in stopping her, but not for long. As her full, falling weight reaches the bottom of its trajectory, the shock of holding nearly nine stone on four fingertips snaps through her shoulder, elbow, and wrist like electric current. Her hand spasms sharply, her fingers jerk uncontrollably, and she lets go, sliding helplessly onwards, face inches from the sandpaper surface, flexing feet scraping fruitlessly. She lands heels-first on the unyielding paving and yelps as the vibration shoots up her legs into her lower back, making both limbs give way and smack her unceremoniously onto her bottom, groaning piteously. Uncontrollable anger surges through her. For fuck's *sake*! She's *sick* of everything being so *difficult*! She's fed up with her *whole* body hurting; and being hot, and sweaty, and *disgusting*! Why can't *anything* go her bloody way for once?! Why does it always have to be such an uphill sodding *struggle*?!

****

Officer Craig pelts down to the Pickford villa as fast as he can, fumbling the keys from his pocket. He stops outside, steadies his breathing, and lets himself in stealthily, easing the door to behind him but not daring to shut it completely. Standing motionless in the hallway, he listens for the slightest sound.

****

She must look an unhinged idiot, sitting here with legs splayed, body slumped, bashing her fists against her own thighs like a toddler having a tantrum.

She shakes her head wearily – what a nutter – and uses the support of the wall to stand, staggering towards the slatted wooden gate at the end of the alley. She can climb it fairly easily, even in her current appalling condition. On the off-chance, she tries the latch, expecting it to be locked. The mechanism resists her determined pressure, then gives abruptly and jerks compliantly loose. Tammi gapes in astonishment. Is Fate finally cutting her a break?

Uncharacteristically, she doesn't pause to consider whether the implausibly-unlocked gate might lead to a Nightingale-staged setup, but hefts it open unhesitatingly, sliding out into the entrance-courtyard beyond.

She tiptoes to the corner of the building and peeks cautiously around it, expecting to see at least one copper standing guard outside her front door; at the very least a squad car parked at the main gate to monitor who goes in and out – but there's no one. The long, elevated walkway that extends along the front of their row of villas is completely empty. What's more, the front door to her home is open! Only an inch or two, but from where she stands, she can see a stripe of familiar hallway paintwork through the gap. Is someone inside or, in the confusion of their forced entry and Marc's probable detention, have the police simply left without remembering to shut it; the responsibility for securing the building delegated down the chain of command like Chinese Whispers until the original task was completely forgotten? How marvellous would that be! She could have a shower and change her clothes, pick up some more money, and equip herself properly for further emergencies with adequate food and drink! There *might* be a copper or two inside awaiting her return…but what if there isn't and she's passing up a golden opportunity? Not everything has to be hard – the compliantly-unlocked gate proves that. There'd be no harm just creeping up to the door and listening…

Tammi steps out of the alley and walks casually, treading lightly, trying to look as if she has as much right and reason to be outside her own front door as on any other day.

****

Officer Craig tiptoes down the entrance hall of the villa, the soles of his shoes make only a slight brushing sound against the tiles. If Mrs Pickford is in here somewhere, will she be able to hear him? He's still out of breath from his sprint. Suppressing the urge to pant makes him feel heady. He needs to be calm; methodical. Breathe normally. Tiptoe a few steps. Pause. Listen. Creep forward a few more. Repeat. Adopting this cautious pattern, he edges up the hall into the living room. All seems just as they had left it, when Detective Alwyn and Agent Nightingale took Pickford off in the Jeep, and the fierce Englishman issued his strict instructions to watch the place like a hawk...

What if he's missed something vital and messed up unforgivably? You had *one job*, he berates himself silently. At least now he's down here, he can check everything thoroughly. If Mrs Pickford is something to do with that dark shape, he might at least be able to redeem his surveillance failure by discovering a pivotal clue. Visibly, nothing in the tidy, minimal living room has moved or disappeared. He zips across to the fridge as quietly as he can, managing to tug open the door with only the slightest chinking-together of the jars nestled on the plastic shelves. The fridge is seemingly too-well-stocked for someone contemplating a moonlight flit. He has no idea whether there's anything missing from it, of course. He's distracted by some decent-looking satay skewers on an uncovered plate. Their spicy scent fills the whole fridge. He wonders whether it's bad form to pinch food from a missing person...and shuts the fridge door with deliberate care before he gets any more stupid ideas. His eyes sweep the floor. No cat food or water. The villa is eerily quiet. He crosses swiftly to the patio doors, scanning the deserted deck. There are no obvious human or feline footprints. He tries the patio door. The handle doesn't budge. It's locked. If Mrs Pickford has returned, she's been careful to cover her tracks. If she's come back for clothes or personal possessions, she's more likely to be in the bedroom than out here. What if she's hiding, waiting for him to leave so she can grab what she needs and escape undetected? It could well have been a cat he saw, or a big seabird – and every minute he spends in here is time when he doesn't have the whole rear of the development under observation from his comfortable eyrie – but the more he thinks about it, the more convinced he becomes that the suspicious movement was on the deck of this property. Until he can be sure, he's got to check the whole place out.

Leaving the living room, he repeats the same process of tiptoe-pause-listen up the passageways to the bedrooms, cautiously and silently approaching the door to the Master Suite.

TWENTY-ONE

Outside her front door, Tammi's ears strain for the slightest sound within. She can't hear voices or detect any footsteps, not even the shuffle of a silent sentry changing position behind the door. The lure of a shower, clean clothes, and something to eat makes her reckless. There's no one here. They've taken Marc, gone in a rush, and left the door. She's going in. She reaches out and gives it a firm push.

****

Fingers on the bedroom door handle, Officer Craig touches his ear to the wood and listens, before depressing it decisively and throwing open the door. An unmade bed. The closets stand ajar, either from where Detective Alwyn checked them earlier, or because Annelisse Pickford is back and he's interrupted her packing. He progresses rapidly from wardrobe to wardrobe, sticking his head in. There's no one hiding in any of them, and they're crammed with clothes, shoes, and other belongings. He crosses to the small bathroom and peers around the door. Empty. It's tidy. Bottles in neat rows on a ledge in the shower. Towels folded over rails. He reaches out and feels the fabric. Dry. Two toothbrushes stand in a mug on the side of the basin. Nothing about this very normal-looking home suggests anyone's going anywhere…yet Agent Nightingale seems convinced the Pickfords are preparing for something. Standing in the centre of the bedroom, he casts around aimlessly for a clue, suddenly spotting the sole of a shoe protruding from beneath the overhanging bedcover. He can't believe he nearly walked away without checking the most obvious hiding place of all! His eight year-old self would be ashamed of him; everyone knows the first place you check for monsters is under the bed.

Officer Craig bends slowly, reaching down, stretching his fingers and getting a secure grip on the covers, preparing to expose the woman cowering beneath the bed with one determined yank. Instead, he makes himself jump as the solitary flip-flop catches in the whipping sheet and flicks upwards into his astounded grasp! It's a huge shoe – a man's size. He tosses it irritably aside and drops to his hands and knees on the bedside runner. There's no one under the bed – just the other massive flip-flop and a couple of curled feathers from the plump pillows. Officer Craig sighs. There's absolutely no one here. He isn't sure whether to be disappointed or relieved. He uses the ornate foot of the carved darkwood bed to haul himself back to his feet, loafing out into the hallway again, no longer concerned about being quiet. He needs to lock up, get back to his vantage point, resume his surveillance, and hope nothing important's happened while he's been wasting time in here. He's just about to round the edge of the wall and walk back down the hall, when he's startled by a solid, thudding sound. It's the front door closing! He inhales sharply, and reverses smartly into the living room, out of sight. Footsteps, soft and light, gradually advance up the hall towards him! He has no radio, no utility belt, no weapon of any kind. He took it all off to make himself more comfortable on his half-hearted stakeout – and came down here in such a panic he'd left it all behind! Holding his breath, he waits for the unexpected visitor to draw level with him, reliant solely on the element of surprise.

****

Tammi glances behind her at the distant sound of a slowing car on the coast road. Even from up here, screened by the ripples of landscaped greenery designed to soften the appearance of the ultra-modern development, she can see through the gently-waving tree branches that it's a police car! For a fraction of a second, Tammi hovers indecisively between leaping inside the villa and locking the door behind her, or finding an alternative hiding place from which to observe this latest worrying development. Realistically, the police are patrolling up here because of her. The last thing she wants is to be in her own shower by the time they bust the door down – perhaps they've even made Marc surrender his keys?

As the car swings off the main road and approaches the front gate of the Smuggler's Bluff development, Tammi drops to a crouch on the walkway, wincing as the tight, congealing cuts on her knees reopen. She scuttles back along to the debateable safety of the alley, hunkering down so low she's practically lying on the tiles.

A single officer driving. He presses the entryphone, waits for the gates to swing smoothly open, and rattles through in a Jimny so comprehensively battered no amount of reflective stripes and official logos can disguise its rickety state. Encouragingly, if it comes to a pursuit down a forest trail, that thing'll never hold together long enough to catch her. It jerks and shudders to the far end of the car park, where the officer gets out and jogs up to one of the most-exclusive bungalows at the highest point of the development. The front door opens as he approaches. He speaks to a woman Tammi can't identify at this distance. She sighs, finally comprehending what's happening here; why no coppers chased her right under the pool and no one was waiting for her when she crawled back out, either. It's all very Nightingale. Be subtle, and sit it out until patience yields its own reward. He's chosen an observation point so high up the cliff it provides an uninterrupted vista of the *entire* hillside to its rear, without alerting her to a noticeable police presence on the development. She should have been able to work it out, really…and if she wasn't panicking so much about time, she probably would have done. Does it mean all her crawling around has been utterly pointless? Has she already been seen, and he's gradually and unobtrusively calling in reinforcements to take appropriate action?

The woman at the villa's front door is pointing – straight at her! – and the Antiguan cop is turning, looking, pointing too…right down towards where she's hiding! Oh God…someone *has* seen her! If they already know she's here, should she confound expectations and slip back through the gate…but go where? To what end? There's already a copper somewhere on that cliff path – she's seen his footprints. There's evidently at least one other on her neighbour's deck high up the hillside, probably with a telescope bigger than Hubble. There *could* plausibly be a whole division of them eating the contents of her fridge right now; waiting, mere metres away, for her to return home and collect all the personal belongings she's regretfully leaving behind. She *can't* go back. She can only go on. The indescribable weight of dread building inside her, Tammi watches the copper take his leave of the woman at the door, turn briskly on his heel, and march swiftly down the shaded, connecting walkways directly towards where she cowers, sick with apprehension. She shrinks back behind the edge of the wall, wriggling into the right-angle between building and gate, as if this will protect her. As the heavy, ringing footsteps get louder, she holds her breath and prays fervently to a God in whom she has no faith for miraculous deliverance from inevitable discovery.

****

Three-two-one-NOW! Officer Craig leaps into the centre of the living room, howling like a banshee…straight into the familiar face of Officer Baptiste, "Aaaaggghhhh! What the *hell* are you trying to do, give me a heart attack?!"

"I'm sorry…I thought you were *her* – the *target!*"

His colleague shakes his head scornfully, "Well, I'm clearly *not*, am I?"

Sheepishly, Craig backs off, muttering, "Sorry…I… Sorry."

"Ok…whatever," Baptiste jerks a thumb, "I've got kit for you in the car."

"Great, thanks." A thought occurs, "Hey, how did you get in here?"

Baptiste responds as if he's an idiot, "The door was wide open!"

"Oh…oh…yeah. That's right." But, he'd left it open the merest crack…? The wind must have caught it.

Baptiste's brows draw together, "Are you ok?"

"Yeah. Yeah, I am… How did you know I'd be down here?"

Baptiste can't disguise his irritation, "What *is* this, interrogation practice?!"

"No...I – "

"I went up to the villa you're *supposed* to be staking out from. The woman there said you'd run down here to check something. Hey, did you really see anything, or did you just need a shit and not want to do it at her place, huh?"

His colleague jabs him playfully in the ribs, and Officer Craig finds himself grinning despite his lingering unease. Baptiste's manner is so relaxed; so untroubled, that he can feel the heavy conviction of having failed in his charge lifting from his body like an oxen released from the ploughman's yoke. It's not his responsibility to catch this woman; it's Agent Nightingale's! This is a British investigation, not an Antiguan one! He just needs to obey orders and stop acting as if he's been abandoned here to apprehend her single-handedly. He's been told to observe and report, so that's what he's going to do.

"Let's get this stuff unloaded then."

Baptiste, evidently reluctant to hurry back to real work, gives the smart living area a cursory once-over, "Nothing actually wrong then?"

"Nah...it's all as we left it earlier."

"I wonder what it's all about?"

"Who knows, man! It's a British Government problem. Nothing to do with us."

"So, what *did* you see?"

Officer Craig shrugs, and loafs to the front door beckoning Baptiste after him, "Oh…a cat. Just a cat. Come on, let's go."

****

The footsteps stop. Tammi opens one eye, half-expecting there to be a copper standing in the mouth of the alley right in front of her, already reaching for his handcuffs…but there's no one there. She struggles back to her feet, shoots to the corner of the wall, and peeks around it, just in time to see the cop disappearing through her front door! Tammi's spent legs nearly give way at the sight. They really *are* all in there waiting for her! To think, she'd nearly walked straight in! She'd opened the door! The only thing that'd stopped her marching confidently up her own hallway was the arrival of that tired little 4x4. The door closes behind the policeman, and Tammi squats back down in the lee of the wall, staring out across the car park towards the main gate, collecting her shaken wits.

Again, she takes a cautious peep. The front door to her villa remains closed. There's still no one stationed on the walkway outside; nor is there anyone obviously watching from anywhere else on the development. Even if there's a cop behind the blinds in every window, they'll still need to mount a pretty fleet pursuit to discover where she's going. This is her chance, and she's got to seize it! She's confident of evading detection if she can get out of the gate and across the main road without being caught. Once into the undergrowth on the other side, she's got a whole island's worth of jungle to hide in. Unless he's made some sort of sneaky deal with Nightingale, only she and Fishmandatu know about the rendezvous point…and Tammi's got another location to visit first – somewhere only she knows. It's therefore impossible for Nightingale to get to her initial port of call before her and mount an ambush. Of *course*! That's *why* he's still here, isn't it, just watching from afar and scratching his head? *All* he's got is Pickford, and poor old Marc doesn't know a thing; she's made sure of it! Now – this moment – is the best chance she's got to make a run for it!

Tammi skids out of the mouth of the alley, crosses the last few yards of tiled walkway at a tiptoeing trot, and charges headlong down the access ramp. She fights her instincts and leans forward, using bodyweight momentum, springing lightly so her running footsteps can't be heard, praying she won't trip and tumble headfirst down the slope. She hits the tarmac at considerable speed, using the impetus she's developed to carry her more than halfway towards the gate before the slight uphill climb kicks in and she's forced to expend greater effort to keep going, driving her little arms like pistons to assist her leaden legs. The pedestrian gate in the front wall of the complex is a turnstile. She jabs the release button with one frantic thumb, diving upon the revolving bars. She gasps in surprise as they spin sharply under the force of her shove, ejecting her smoothly out onto the tarmacked roadway like a chocolate bar from a vending machine. She deliberately doesn't turn to check behind her – she hasn't a second to waste, and doesn't want to gift the gate-cam a clear image of her face – but thunders across the deserted road and dives straight into the dense rainforest on the other side, making for a hiking trail half a mile to the east.

One moment, the path of the fugitive is obvious. The tall grasses by the roadside wave and dip crazily as she plunges through them.

A low-hanging branch of Whitewood jerks and bounces as it's thrust aside. Then, just as quickly, what's swaying the grass is only a gust of tropical wind. What's bobbing the branches is merely the flapping launch of a cawing jungle bird. The protective embrace of the forest closes around the diminutive figure, and she's gone.

TWENTY-TWO

Nodding in the muggy shade, an unexpected sound rouses the sluggish Fishmandatu. He jerks his head up, self-consciously wiping drool from his bottom lip, yawning wide to suck in some oxygen. It's *so hot*. A thunderhead is building far out to sea. If it breaks by tonight, at least it might relieve this stifling humidity. The sound that alerted him is a woman stepping on to the rickety pontoon and making the storm-shattered planks crack beneath her feet. Fishmandatu checks his watch – a little over five minutes to spare. That's cutting it fine, even for his cocksure co-conspirator. The sun's so bright, she's just a black silhouette against the blue sea, but he knows it's Rivers. Her shape; her gait; her mannerisms – all so familiar to a man who'd worshipped her identical twin for most of his adult life. If *only* it could be Annelisse he's padding out of the jungle towards. If *only* the little backpack she carries could be a papoose in which their forbidden, forgotten baby sleeps soundly. The beginnings of a sob bring Fishmandatu up short, halfway down the sand. By the time he collects himself, she's noticed his presence and advances to meet him. The illusion shatters. Only perturbing reality remains.

The closer he gets, the clearer it becomes that she's filthy! She's so comprehensively smeared in dust she resembles a Victorian coal-miner; clear, bright eyes shining from a grime-caked face. She's cut, grazed, bruised – all a result of a close-encounter with the man in the light-grey suit? He gapes, blurting tactlessly, "What happened to you?"

She shakes her head irritably, as if the question is superfluous, and grunts, "I fell down a manhole. Where were you?"

He gestures vaguely back up the beach, "Waiting in the shade. It's too hot." He looks pointedly at his watch, "Cutting it a bit fine?"

She glares at him, "Am I late?"

"No…"

"Well, then!"

He steps up onto the pontoon. The ancient wood creaks alarmingly, and several of the loosened planks slide sharply sideways under his weight, "Christ! Is this thing going to stay up?"

She smirks sarcastically, "I expect so, Phillip – just don't practice your tap-dancing."

They face-off in the full sun, the intense heat cranking up the tension until the air seems to crackle around them. Fishmandatu can't let on he saw her this morning. She'll immediately want to know what took him to the beach beneath Smuggler's Bluff, and he can't betray his knowledge of the dark-haired man and the professional theft of the folder from the safe…not yet. Not until he's on that plane and can't easily be removed. Tammi – exhausted, thirsty, sore all over – can't ask whether Fishmandatu was watching her villa this morning, right before Nightingale's arrival. She can't yet risk accusing him of being in league with M I 5…not until the precious folder is safely in her possession.

His backpack makes his shoulder sweat. He swings it to the deck. She doesn't take her eyes off it until it's sitting at his feet like a loyal hound, whereupon she fixes him with her penetrating stare, and demands, "Folder. Please. As we arranged."

Fishmandatu prudently avoids eye contact and scans the horizon, "Not yet. Where's the plane? As we 'arranged'."

She pouts, looks tetchily at her watch, and snaps, "It'll be here. *Folder.*"

"*No.* When I see the plane."

Tammi snarls aggressively, "You'd better not be messing me around, Phillip!"

He kisses his teeth contemptuously, "Likewise."

She's about to retort when he sees her expressive eyes widen in alarm, mouth dropping open. She breathes, "What the fuck is *this*...?" She's not looking at him, but at something over his left shoulder. Wary of a trick, Phillip risks the speediest of glances behind him, and jerks in horror.

A filthy, sweat-soaked man lurches out of the jungle and staggers down the thin strip of sand towards them.

TWENTY-THREE

Nathan.

He almost trips clambering from the sand onto the unstable pontoon, face twisting with hatred as he hisses, "Going somewhere, Fishy?"

"Nate…"

Her furious voice behind him, an insistent tug at the sleeve of his t-shirt, "You *know* this clown? Is this something to do with you? Who the hell else have you spilled your guts to, eh? Is the *whole* fucking *island* about to turn up, or what?"

"Just shut up for a minute!"

Over the noise of the wind in the trees and the breaking waves, Fishmandatu's ears have caught the low burble of an aircraft's engine. The faint black dot emerges from the building storm cloud, gradually becoming a triangle, a cross, and finally the defined shape of fuselage and wings. The little plane throttles back sharply, and the skis hit, bounce, hit, skim, and eventually float with engineered precision across the glistening surface of the sea. All three watch it turn in an elegant circle out on the flatter water, and begin to taxi slowly towards them. Fishmandatu points agitatedly, "Nate, the plane's here, see? I told you I'd get us out, didn't I? You can come with me. Perfect timing, man!"

Nathan's dark eyes are empty of their usual mischievous glint. His voice, normally rich with animation, is disturbingly flat, monotone;

dead, "You're not going anywhere, Fishy. Not now. It's too late. You've done too much. Your journey's over, pal. It ends today...and I'm going to be the one who finishes it."

Distressed, Fishmandatu wheedles, "Nate, please...don't talk like that. I'm going to my kids. To my *kids*, Nate! Dee'll be there. I've sorted it. Amanda too. Just get on this plane with me! We're getting out of here, away from Chadwick. It's over, Nate! He can't *ever* touch us again!"

"Oh Fishy...you are clueless. You'll be seeing Dee and Amanda long before I do, but only in passing. They'll be floating up as you're dropping down. Enjoyed the climate here, have you, Fishy? I hope so...because it's going to be fucking hot where you'll end up, you evil, murdering bastard."

"What are you *saying*? I haven't *murdered* anyone!"

"Of *course* you have, Fishy. My wonderful wife...my beautiful daughter – "

"How can I possibly have – ?"

"He bugs my 'phones, man! He listens to every damn conversation we have, from the mother-in-law whining about her corns to the bloke trying to sell us double-glazing...and *you* got Simone to ring Dionne, didn't you...on a *bugged line*! Chadwick will have heard *Every Single Word*!"

"Oh shit..." Fishmandatu's legs buckle. He staggers backwards and nearly falls, reaching for one of the pontoon uprights to steady his swoon and recover his feet.

There's suddenly something in Nathan's hand that catches the sunlight and flashes blindingly. The gun.

Nate's creeping unsteadily across the bowing planks with grim determination, growling, "Oh shit indeed, Fishy. I'd be very surprised if any of them are still breathing – your precious kids included...not that you really give a shit about them one way or another, eh? Easy come, easy go. You can just get a new bird and have some more, right? You've as good as killed 'em all...and now I'm going to kill you."

Aghast, Fishmandatu croaks, "No, Nate, *no*! *Please*! Come with us! We don't *know* they're dead! There's a chance they got away, Nate! There's *always* a chance...you should *never* give up!"

Still slithering across the silvered wood of the creaking pontoon as fast as his erstwhile friend backs away, Nathan scoffs incredulously at the absurdity of the idea, too maddened by grief to listen to reason. Instead, he stiffens his arm, takes aim – "NO, Nate! *Please*! NO! We're *mates*! *NATHAN*!" – and fires directly at the dismayed face of Phillip Fishmandatu.

TWENTY-FOUR

At the very moment Nathan squares his stance to shoot, the rotten board beneath his right foot gives way, his leg dropping straight through the pontoon and his body lurching, the zipping bullet flying wide of its target. Fishmandatu throws himself to the deck the moment he realises Nathan really is going to fire. He hears the bullet pass close, doesn't see it; is only thankful it's missed him. As Nathan falls, the gun tumbles from his grasp and skitters away across the weathered wood, out of easy reach. Nathan squeals as the serrated edge of the snapped plank shaves his shin down to the bone, instantly dropping to his left knee and trying to pull his trapped right leg back through the jagged hole without injuring it further. Fishmandatu dives and shoves Nathan aggressively backwards. Nate screams again as the sharp wood slices the ligament at the back of his knee, drawing further blood. He tumbles sideways, one leg still painfully pinned, the other splayed uselessly across the deck. Scurrying past the helpless Nathan, Fishmandatu reaches the gun, snatches it up, thumps to his knees behind his old colleague, grips him in a powerful headlock, and presses the barrel of the .22 pistol hard against Nathan's temple.

"Fucking sit still, Nate…or I'll use this!"

Panting with the agony in his lacerated leg, Nathan's struggles temporarily cease. Shuddering with shock, Fishmandatu keeps as firm a hold as he can upon his gasping, grunting prisoner, and glances anxiously up at Tammi's appalled expression. For a moment, they simply stare at one another. She opens her mouth to speak, but is silenced by the abrupt throttling-up of the seaplane engine. Head snapping round, she beholds the horrified face of the pilot through the cockpit window, still several feet from the end of the pontoon, clearly evaluating the troubling tableau before him and concluding this latest booking isn't worth the fee. Instead of a final approach to embark his passengers, the plane begins to turn the opposite way, back out to sea.

Tammi doesn't hesitate, but sprints down the lethally-unstable pontoon after the obviously-departing aircraft, waving her arms and screeching frantically, "No! No! *Wait*! We had a *deal*! You *can't go*! *Waaaait*! *Pleeeease*!"

Fishmandatu can only gape in astonishment as she throws herself into the sea with desperate recklessness, little rucksack strapped to her back like the shell on a crustacean. She hits the water with an inelegant smack and instantly drives away with all her might, skinny arms slapping, little feet kicking. She keeps swimming with doughty determination towards the seaplane, though it's apparent it won't wait around for her to reach it. The burbling engine note is building, speed increasing as it completes its 180° turn, hops a couple of times off the disturbed surface of the water, then finally leaps, lifts, catches the currents of air, and soars away. Rivers' head is a small, golden dot in the huge expanse of blue, the wake of take-off washing backwards and submerging her.

Nathan chooses that moment to retaliate, twisting despite the phenomenal pain the movement causes, roaring and driving his elbow directly into Fishmandatu's stomach, taking him by surprise. Fishmandatu topples backwards, knuckles whacking the deck as he falls, the gun bouncing free and rolling away. The weight of Nate's body thuds hard on top of him as his old friend strains every sinew to reach the pistol first, crying out in frustration as his fingers grope mere centimetres away. Desperate, Fishmandatu throws out a hand, feels for the gun, grasps it firmly and, before he has time to consider the grossness of his action, cracks the butt against the side of Nathan's skull with all his might. Nate makes a strange, strangled noise in his throat, swaying just enough for Fishmandatu to crawl from underneath him. By the time he's on his feet, Nate's recovered sufficiently to make a grab for Phillip's legs. He dances away, skidding on the splintering planks, nearly falling again as several give way around him and tumble into the dark water below. As Nate bends to a frantic fresh attempt to free his impaled leg, Fishmandatu springs forward and brings the butt of the gun down on the back of Nathan's head once; twice; thrice; the sickening sound reminding him of cracking an eggshell with a teaspoon. Nathan collapses across the deck, eyes rolling, mouth slack, head lolling to one side, dark blood glistening in his black hair.

Phillip doesn't linger over Nathan's prone form, but turns and staggers up the pontoon as fast as his trembling legs can carry him, clumsily shoving the gun into the waistband of his shorts, calling, "*TAMMI!*" at the top of his voice, head tracking from side to side, searching for the blonde hair in the blue water. At the end of the structure he drops to hands and knees, hanging over the edge and quickly surveying the area directly beneath in case she's swum back and is clinging to one of the legs, strength spent, unable to haul herself out.

There's no sign of her.

Lifting his head, he tries to be methodical despite his mounting distress, scanning steadily left to right, endeavouring not to miss a single inch of gently-rolling ocean. He shouts again and again; yelling her name; screaming it...but there's no reply. Tammi is gone.

Distraught; unaccountably bereft; Fishmandatu rocks back on his heels at the pontoon's edge, and howls his desolation at the merciless sun. It feels like losing Annelisse all over again. Powerless against the onslaught of emotion, he flops forward to hands and knees, sobbing until he can barely breathe. As his heaving cries lessen to hiccupping moans, he becomes conscious of coolness in the small of his sweating back; a distinct loosening of the waistband of his shorts, as if...? Befuddled by anguish, he rummages uncertainly behind him with fingers that don't feel like his own, probing blindly for the pistol. It's not there!

Distressed; confused; he whirls around and something hard, cold, and metallic smacks against his cheekbone, startling him.

"Sorry, Phillip, but you and your unhinged mate ballsed-up my plan."

He has no time to react. It's over for Phillip Fishmandatu before he's even drawn sufficient breath to plead for mercy. Features all-but-obliterated by the close-quarters shot, the lifeless body tips backwards off the pontoon and floats briefly on the surface of the glittering water, before tangling in the swirling undercurrents and starting to sink.

Not given to sentimentality, Tammi's dripping figure turns from unemotional observation of her former ally to deal with the other obstacle that's arrived suddenly and inconveniently in her path. If there was any justice in this bloody world, she'd be halfway to Montserrat by now!

She skids up the deck to the comatose Nathan Palmer. Taking care not to touch the body, a few energetic, heel-first stamps like a cowgirl at a Hoedown are sufficient to splinter and snap the rotten wood surrounding him. Dispassionately, she awaits the inevitable consequence of this strategic damage. It doesn't take long. The dead weight of the unconscious body applies unremitting pressure to the thoroughly-weakened wood until it cracks like melting ice on the surface of a lake, dropping Nathan into the slimy blackness beneath the pontoon with barely a splash. She tosses the gun in after him; she'll never get that through an airport metal detector.

She swivels efficiently on the balls of her feet and grabs at Fishmandatu's rucksack, unzipping and upending it onto the planks. A half-consumed bottle of water. A couple of small packets of crisps. A sponge bag. A change or two of clothes. A small, battered envelope she's pleased to discover contains a float of Eastern Caribbean dollars. She pockets it without hesitation. Fishmandatu's passport. She chucks that into the water too. A charger for a mobile 'phone…but no evidence of the handset. It's probably in his pocket, useless to anyone now. Shame. A mobile 'phone would have come in handy. Where's the bloody *folder*?!

She shakes the discarded clothes increasingly frantically, even though she knows they're not concealing anything. It's bulky, cumbersome, hard to hide. It must be three inches thick – too big to conceal in a lining. There aren't any secret pockets in the backpack. It isn't fucking *here*, is it?! What's the slippery bastard done with it?

Panicking now, she shoves everything back into the bag, zips it shut, and pushes it hurriedly through the large hole in the deck. Folder or no folder, she's got to get off this beach before that pilot has time to radio anyone and report what he's just witnessed.

Standing, she dusts off her hands, rubs gingerly at the circles of sand stuck to her swollen, throbbing knees, and surveys the scene a final time to ensure she's left no evidence of her presence.

With a sigh that might be irritation, frustration, exhaustion, perhaps even regret, Tammi Rivers turns inland once more, and disappears into the thick jungle bordering the deserted beach.

TO BE CONTINUED …

Printed in Great Britain
by Amazon

64949681R00130